DISCARD

THE 40 YEAR SPANN of WVON

Published by National Academy of Blues
3350 So. Kedzie
Chicago, IL 60623

ISBN 0-97465380-2

10 9 8 7 6 5 4 3 2 1

First Edition

This book is dedicated to the memory
of "The Mad Lad," E. Rodney Jones

Preface

At the time of writing of The 40 Year Spann of WVON, E. Rodney Jones, one of the original "Good Guys" at the radio station was alive. Between then and the time we actually went to press, he, unfortunately, passed away.

We, the authors, decided to hold the book back from printing to add more insight into Rodney's character. Of course, he is discussed throughout the book, as all of the "Good Guys" are. As a matter of fact, snippets from the last conversation he had with his partner and long time friend, me, Pervis Spann, is recorded between these pages. We still felt, however, the true significance of his personality in the world of radio was not fully captured. Indeed, how could it be? A man of such dynamic strength, force, and power in the music industry could not be captured in the pages of any novel.

Power. I"ve never seen anybody with as much power as Rodney, when it came to the entertainment world. His influence in the entertainment industry touched such super stars as Sammy Davis Jr., Nancy Wilson, Louis Jordan, Count Bassie, Dakota Staton, Dinah Washington, Otis Redding, Rufus Thomas, Issac Hayes, Gladys Knight, Smokey Robinson, Marvin Gaye, Chuck Jackson, Count Bassie, Joe Williams, Gene Chandler, Jerry Butler, Tyrone Davis, The Chi-lites, The Temptations, Joanne Garrett, The Dells, BB King, Bobby "Blue" Bland, Joe Simone, The Isley Brothers, Wilson Pickett, Jr. Walker and The All Stars, Betty Wright, The Four Tops, The Delfonics, Aretha Franklin, and Shirley Brown.

These are just a few of the thousands of entertainers Rodney helped. Your wildest imagination would not lead you to believe the magnitude of the influence that E. Rodney Jones had on Black entertainment. All the major record labels looked for Rodney's input as to which artist's records would become hits, and Rodney was always right. He had the uncanny ability to know which record and artist would make it and which wouldn't.

While talking to our other partner Verlene Blackburn about Rodney, she reminded me of one particular incident. It was at the Burning Spear, the nightclub we owned together on the south side of Chicago. One evening Rodney came in with an unknown group called Wayne Newton and the CC Riders. He had seen them perform at another club. They were a new act, and Rodney saw the potential. As Verelene said, Rodney was the P. R. man, but I was the boss. I vetoed his decision to have Wayne Newton perform, and as Rodney knew what would happen did. Years later, Wayne blew up. This was not unusual.

Verlene also remembered it was Rodney who made the Park West, a club on the north side a success. At that time, we were the only ones bringing any successful acts to Chicago. He showed the then owners, a couple of Jewish guys, brothers, how to bring in acts and book shows. This led to the creation of "Ticketmaster."

Rodney was a very personable gentleman. When asked what one word would describe E. Rodney Jones, Richard Pegue, one of the "Good Guys" to arrive at the station years later, said he needed more than one word. In the end, he surmised it by saying, Rodney was bigger than big. All of the "Good Guys" were big when Richard hit the scene, but he remembered Rodney as being the biggest of the bunch.

Al Bell, former owner of Stax Records, remembers E. Rodney Jones as a dear, dear, personal friend. Al first bought Stax when it was a production company owned by Jim Stewart and Estelle Axton. The "Ste" of Stewart and the "Ax" in Axton thus created "Stax." Rodney was instrumental in promoting the careers of Stax legends such as Johnny Taylor, Otis Redding, Sam & Dave, Booker T. and the MGs, Carla and Rufus Thomas, William Bell, The Barkays, Lil' Milton, Albert King, Billy Eckstine, The Emotions, The Dramatics, and the Staple Singers. Al actually wrote "I'll Take You There," and Rodney indeed took it there, way up there. Chicago became a backyard to Stax. Rodney was the greatest friend a record company could have.

He really cared about artist and music. The reason Jesse Jackson and Al Bell became hooked up was because of Rodney. Al remembered a call he got from Rodney.

"Al," he said, "there's a guy you've got to meet, because he sounds a lot like you talking about Black empowerment."

After meeting Jesse and hearing his message, Al went on to record "I Am Somebody," an album by Jesse on Stax Records.

VI

Rodney exhibited Black leadership at the level of a Jesse Jackson and a Martin Luther King, Al recalls, just in a different way.

Another incident that's pretty humorous Al tells about Rodney has to do with his love of food. Earl's Hot Biscuits truck stop located in Memphis was one of Rodney's favorite stops. He loved the ham and red eye gravy, grits and biscuits.   Back then, Rodney would call Al and tell him he called the restaurant and placed an order. Al would then have someone pick up Rodney's order, and send it via Delta airlines to Chicago. On this end, Rodney would have it picked up, and delivered to the radio station. This happened on more than one occasion. Rodney would then call Al and tell him he wished he was there to enjoy it with him.

The significance of Rodney in the industry cannot totally be measured. He was one of a kind and will never be forgotten in the music world. He was a founding member of the radio disc jockey's union. Long before EF Hutton, when Rodney spoke, people listened. The Burning Spear owned a boat dubbed The Mad Lad, named after Rodney. It was docked right across from Navy Pier. They partied so hard on that boat, it finally sank.

Rodney's power over the record industry has never been equaled. In the pages of this novel, you will discover this and more. With the passing of E. Rodney Jones, America has truly lost a legend.

ACKNOWLEDGEMENTS

I would like to thank Lucky Cordell, Don Cornelious, Herb Kent, Richard Pegue, George O'Hare, Cliff Kelley, E. Rodney Jones, and Verlene Blackburn for their revealing interviews.

I also would like to give my sincerest regards to Leroy Phillips, for allowing me to use pictures from his extensive collection, and to BB King for his major contribution to this project.

My thanks goes out to Dr. Jerald Walker, Professor at Bridgewater University for his details to the obvious.

I can't forget to thank Frank Mitchell one of the best Graphic Designers in the business.

Also, my deepest gratitude goes out to Hermene Hartman, who, as editor, took the time out of her busy schedule, to use her journalism expertise to give this book the right polish.

Last but not least, my thanks goes out to the millions of fans and friends, who without, this book would not be possible.

Foreward

PERVIS (BLUESMAN) SPANN is truly a living legend. Over the course of his life, Pervis has mastered the art of being "a jack of all trades." An entrepreneur concert promoter, legendary radio personality, steel mill worker, cab driver, and electronic engineer are many of the hats he has worn over the course of his professional life; but, what he is best at is being Daddy.

The true essence of a man lies in the fruit that he bears. I am proud to be the daughter of "The Bluesman". He has managed to defy all odds to reach his pinnacle of success. Born in Itta Bena, Mississippi, Daddy picked enough cotton to become one of the richest men in Itta Bena. While we commend him for it now, that was the kind of work ethic that could get you killed in the South back in the '50's. He was not trying to be a trailblazer, but that is who my Daddy is, a hard worker who believes there is nothing he cannot achieve.

As most parents, Daddy always wanted us to have more than he was given as a child. He stressed education for all of us. It was a mandate. As I have grown older, I have come to realize that commitment to what you do and vision to go beyond that which is tangible is the gift that Daddy has given to all four of us.

Any success that my siblings or I may achieve has little to do with our individual accomplishments, strokes of genius, or self-aggrandizement. Our success lies in having a role model who in his own unorthodox way achieved more than most, and who taught his children that our birthright is to do the same.

His contribution to the earth may not be truly appreciated until he has long passed away; however, Daddy's story is a great one. No one book can tell it all. He is a walking encyclopedia on life's lessons. Consider this Volume One.

Enjoy!

Melody Spann-Cooper
President and General Manager, WVON Radio

President Bill Clinton and Pervis Spann at the White House

XIII

Introduction

When Pervis Spann first approached me to assist him in writing this novel, my initial thought was how flattered I was to be trusted to help depict a story of such epic proportion.

As I talked to 'The Blues Man', and interviewed some of the other Good Guys, I began to imagine myself traveling back and forth through time, as if the machine I was in made different stops randomly, depending on which button was pushed, similar to the H.G. Wells classic. With that in mind, we decided to write this book in that same manner.

This is a story told in parallel time, with the same characters, but from different eras. We invite the readers to live vicariously through the pages and relive the glory days.

Many readers lived these days and will be able to relate to the different experiences told in these pages. So, kick back and relax in your journey in The 40 Year Spann of WVON time machine.

Linda C. Walker

Prologue

Sitting in The Soul Queen, a popular restaurant on the south side of Chicago, Pervis Spann, affectionately known as "The Blues Man" put another fork full of greens in his mouth. He thought back over his long career in radio, "I could've been at the bottom of Lake Michigan if I had not taken special care of my actions", he said out loud, but to himself, a habit he had picked up lately. He finished his peach cobbler, gathered his hat and keys, paid the bill, and got in his 1950 Chevy. It was a cold night and the Windy City was living up to its name, a lot different from the night he drove into the parking lot of WVON for the first time some 40 years ago. Mentally, he took that same drive again.

April 1, 1963, to Pervis, was just another day. The one thing different though, was that this was his first day at WVON, the Voice of the Negro, a new radio station with a Black format, the first of its kind in Chicago. A day of firsts. He was the first disc jockey to kick off the programming that day since he started at midnight. It was a new gig, but the same duties. He was a disc jockey at station WOPA in Oak Park spinning the blues. In fact, that's how he came to know the new owners of WVON. Pervis thought back on a revelation Leonard recounted to him some time ago.

♫ ♫ ♫

Leonard Chess walked into the junkyard he owned with his brother on 29th and State Street in Chicago.

"Hey Phil, what's going on?" Leonard asked, entering the office they shared as he pulled up a chair.

"Oh nothing much. I was thinking about going across the street to that church over there," Phil answered.

"Church? Since when did you become religious?" Leonard inquired in amazement. From the time their parents brought them over from Poland as immigrants, he had never known Phil to have any interest in church.

"Every since I got an ear full of that choir. It's amazing," Phil answered. "Why don't you come with me and see, I mean hear for yourself."

"In this all Black neighborhood, do you think they'd welcome a couple of Jewish guys?" Leonard questioned.

"Yes. I've been over there a few times already. They're very friendly," Phil replied as he stood to leave.

"Okay, I think I will join you."

They strolled across the street to the Baptist church, took a seat in the pew and settled down to become divinely inspired.

Leonard was not prepared for the foot tapping praise he was about to receive. He began sliding down the bench,

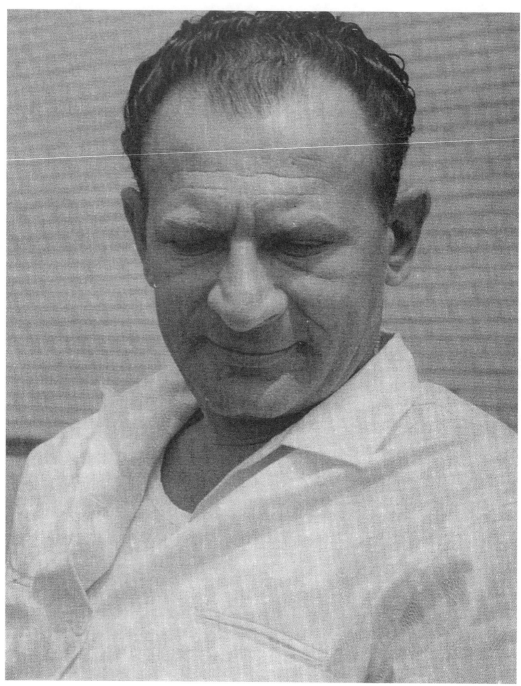

Leonard Chess

being unconsciously drawn closer to the scent of Chanel #5 from a hat bedecked madam, reeking pleasant havoc on his nostrils. Phil, on the other hand, immediately leapt to his feet to join in the worship, clapping his hands and singing the now familiar hymnals.

Just as the choir begin to lift their voices and sing the third song in a row, one of the members broke out in a hoofed tattoo that ended in the rhythmnic beat signaling the catching of the 'Holy Ghost.' Another choir member produced a tambourine. After several moments of seemingly uncontrollable gyrations and mercy pleading outcries, other members of the choir began to carry the smitten member out. Leonard felt as if something had taken over his own soul. He saw a glorious light in his mind's eye and listened to that little voice, just as the pastor began his sermon on the power of faith.

Two and a half hours later, as they walked back to their junkyard, Leonard said, "You know Phil, you were right. That choir sang beautifully, and you know what else? I had an inspiration while I was there --" Leonard suddenly stopped talking, and stood still.

"What kind of --"

"Shhh," Leonard whispered, "be quiet." He placed a hand on Phil's arm and didn't move.

"What is it?" Phil asked, sotto voiced.

"That singing, where is it coming from?" Leonard whispered back.

They stood there silent as the Sunday afternoon breeze, like a magic carpet, carried a harmony so sweet throughout the stratosphere, that both men smiled unconsciously as one of their senses tingled.

"Come on, Phil," Leonard said, just as abruptly as he requested silence a few minutes ago, and grabbed his brother's arm.

"Where are we going?" Phil asked as he was being ushered non too gently down the sidewalk.

"Follow that voice," Leonard replied as his ears, like a Doberman listening to a possible intruder, zeroed in on the music's direction.

Just around the corner from their shop, a group of young men stood, crooning in the sunshine.

"Doo wap woo . . .," came from the trio.

As Leonard and Phil joined a gathering crowd, the men continued their

4

impromptu concert. They stood out there at least 45 minutes listening as a different singer took the lead. At one point somebody broke out a harmonica and added a bluesy flavor to the music.

After the wild applause that followed the sad but soothing scene, Leonard walked up to one of the performers.

"Hello, I'm Leonard Chess. You guys really got something going on here. This is my brother Phil," he said as he held out a hand in greeting and motioned to his brother standing by his side.

"What it is, man." The gentleman speaking slapped five on Leonard's outstretched hand and continued, "I'm, Willie Dixon. This here cat is known as Howlin' Wolf, and over there is Lil' Walter."

"I'm pleased to meet you gentlemen," Leonard responded. He went on to say, "here's my card, Willie. My brother and I own a liquor store on 39th and Cottage Grove, Chess Liquors, with a bar in the back. Why don't you guys stop by tomorrow? I could use some good acts in the bar area."

"Dig it," Willie answered in the affirmative, and turned to talk to a lady tugging at his sleeve.

Leonard and Phil left the group, and headed back to the junk yard. As they walked, Leonard filled his brother in on his inspiration.

"It came to me as we sat in church, then it was confirmed as we left. Let's get a record company."

"A what? Are you crazy. We don't know how to run a record company," Phil protested, but he felt excitement building nevertheless.

"So we'll learn. We already have that lounge in the back of the store on Cottage, and you and I both have an ear for music. Let's use some of that money we have invested in the stock market that Dad left us, and let others have the opportunity to hear what we just heard, and be able buy it."

"You know, Leonard, I think you're on to something," Phil said.

From that point on, things began to happen fast. At first, Phil and Leonard began to have Black artists perform at their lounge right behind the store. Then they formed Chess Records, a big blues label, sprinkled with jazz.

Well into the new project, Phil, who took to the record company like a fish to water entered their new offices located on 21st and Michigan Avenue. They were fortunate to get a spot on Record Row. At that time, 1962, from 21st street to around 13th on Michigan was called Record Row, consisting of Ernie Leaner, Jimmie Martin, Bill Southstone, Vee Jay Records and Chess.

Phil, who handled most of the recordings, entered Leonard's office and waited until he finished the call he was on. Leonard handled the business and Phil needed some questions answered.

Leonard hung up the receiver and asked, "Phil, what brings you here?"

"Well I was just wondering how the numbers are looking. We constantly pack the bar because of our music. Blacks are minorities just like us, and we can relate to people trying to better themselves. We've been recording their records, and been selling them like crazy at the lounge, so I'm sure the artists are happy. It just seems we should be able to reach a larger audience. It'll help them and us at the same time," Phil said.

"My sentiments exactly," Leonard agreed. "It's true the more people who hear our artist, the more people buy our records. Sales are okay, but they could be better. I went over to some of the radio stations to try to get them to play our records, but they said no way. They wouldn't hear of playing Black people's music. The only station that agreed to play some was WGES. Al Benson, the number one Black disc jockey in Chicago, or maybe in America will play some, and a few of the other DJs over there. I also have to talk to some people at WOPA in Oak Park. A guy they call 'Big' Bill Hill is over there, and a couple of others."

"I was just wondering. You know you were always the better figure head than I," Phil said. "Oh yea, by the way, there are some jazz artists I'm thinking about recording that you might like. One's named Ramsey Lewis. Another one is a great talent by the name of Gene Ammons, then there's a lady, Etta James you might like." Phil knew Leonard had always been a ladies man, though he had to admit once he got married and had a son, Marshall, Leonard had slowed down considerably.

"Okay, just let me know when and where," Leonard responded.

The next morning, Leonard went to WOPA in Oak Park. He knew

about Big Bill Hill, and he also heard about something called the "All Night Round Up" that a DJ named McKee Fitzhugh used to broadcast from several lounges. McKee had someone named Pervis Spann on as a regular guest with a smooth voice, a perfect intro for the blues.

"Hello," Leonard said to a pretty receptionist behind a sliding glass wall. "You're looking very lovely this morning. Is there a gentleman by the name of McKee Fitzhugh available?" he asked.

"No. I've been informed Mr. Fitzhugh will not be returning. Mr. Pervis Spann is to handle all his inquiries, but he isn't in now. Is there a number he can reach you?" she questioned

Leonard reached in his pocket, handed her his card with a wink, and left. Later on that day, Leonard received a call from Pervis Spann. It turned out the owner of WOPA decided that McKee Fitzhugh had lost interest in that show, and gave it to Pervis. Now, instead of it being the McKee "All Night Round Up," it turned out to be the Blues Man, Pervis Spann's "All Night Round Up." Pervis only broadcast from one location, but he was on WOPA five days a week.

"Pervis, can you stop by my office tomorrow? I have some records I'm sure your listeners would love," Leonard asked.

They agreed to meet, and from then on had a very mutually satisfactory business relationship. By Pervis playing blues, and being "The Blues Man" and Leonard recording blues, Pervis became very important to him.

This went on for some time. Different DJs would stop by Chess Records and pick up some tunes to play on the air. Al Benson over at WGES was on during drive time, and he was able to sell some records for Chess. Besides Pervis, these were the only people Leonard Chess could get to play his records. They had another guy at WGES by the name of Ric Ricardo who had a slogan, "Rock with Ric." He was on in the mornings. Then at noon they had, Richard Stamz. He had a theme song that went something like this, "Open the door Richard. Open the door Richard and let me in. Open the door Richard. Richard why don't you open that door," accompanied by a very funny verse and sultry saxophone. Then, Richard would come in and start talking. He was only on the air for an hour, but there were so many Blacks in Chicago, even an hour would give a person great visibility. And it did for Richard Stamz.

"You know Phil," Leonard said to his brother one evening at the office after everyone was gone for the day except those two, "I'm just not satisfied with the amount of sales we're getting. I talked to all the radio stations in the Chicagoland area, and I still can't get any but 'GES and 'OPA to play our records. The Ol' Swing Master Al Benson at WOPA is only on for three hours, but every record he plays for us turns out to be a hit. I was talking to a DJ the other day by the name of Herb Kent. He works at WHFC. He said the owners at that station might be selling it. I asked him to set up a meeting with me and the owner, a congressman by the name of Hoffman. I didn't mention it to you before now because I hadn't heard anything else from Kent, that is until today. He set it up for the congressman and me to have lunch next week. I'm thinking about buying that station so that we can be sure to get our records played."

Phil sat staring at his brother with his mouth hung open. "You want us to buy a radio station? Are you sure?" he asked.

"Since we're recording blues, and Chicago, being the market that it is as far as blues is concerned, why not? This is the prime spot to buy a radio station," Leonard said.

"Leonard, there was a time when I would have thought you were crazy, but it makes since. If we own our own station, we can play our own records, and make some money too. It sounds like a good idea. I'm going to leave all the details to you. Count me in."

Chess Records was recording all the best blues around, and in negotiations to buy a radio station. Things were beginning to look pretty good for the Chess brothers, until the calls started coming in.

At first Leonard paid them no attention. He just considered them prank calls. Nowadays, one could expect just about anything to happen. Then they started coming more regularly and more menacingly.

"Chess," came the gruff voice, one day. "We want in on the action. We understand you're about to monopolize the record and radio industry among the Negroes. We want in."

"Who is this?" Leonard demanded.

"Never mind. This is how it's going to work. We'll send a messenger over every Friday. Based on arbitron ratings and record sales, they'll be a note to you with the amount you're to 'donate' to the cause. Put cash in an envelope and give it back to him. Just consider us as your security. Business men of your caliber will need protection."

"I'm not going to go along with your blackmail. I'm calling the police," Leonard said into the receiver.

"You'll be sorry." Click, then silence.

Actually, Leonard had no intention of calling the police. He had somebody else to call. He picked up the receiver and dialed a number.

"Hello Hymmie? This is Leonard. Listen, I need you to check something out. . ."

 The next few weeks were pretty hectic. Leonard had his hands full with trying to line up DJs for his yet to be acquired new radio station. No more calls came from the mysterious caller, and Leonard relaxed. He knew if anybody could handle the situation, it would be Hymmie Weiss. He didn't tell Phil because he knew his temper.

During Leonard's maneuvers to secure proper on air talent, the deal between Congressman Hoffman and himself became a reality. The congressman agreed to sell Leonard the AM station, WHFC, for $1 million. Hoffman also had an FM signal. The FM signals really didn't mean much at the time. AM was the king of the radio. When Hoffman sold him the AM station, rather than pay the light bill on the FM, he included it in the deal, just through it in for a dollar. The FM signal then was WSDM, which stood for 'smack dab in the middle'.

Leonard was pleased with his acquisition.

"We're able to cover most of the Black people in Chicago," he excitedly explained to Phil the next day. "Blacks had not really penetrated the suburbs too much, so even at night, the station would cover the whole city where all the Negroes live."

"How are the new disc jockeys coming along?"

"Not bad. Tomorrow I meet with Pervis Spann, the all night blues man from WOPA."

Rolling back to the present, and into the WVON parking lot, Pervis mentally noted the change of the driveway entrance that had taken place a few years ago, and thought about a few other changes. One being that now in 2003, the WVON format is basically one of talk radio, as opposed to that of rhythm and blues of the 60's, & 70's.

Blues had always been Pervis' first love. He entered his office, checked his messages and sat back on the tan leather sofa. Glancing at his watch, he noticed he still had a couple of hours before his still popular blues show would air. Kicking back, he remembered how Leonard Chess singled him out to be WVON's first blues man.

Back in 1963, Mr. Chess called him to come down to his record company. Pervis went down to talk to him, even though he was at WOPA, and doing very well playing blues and playing Chess records. Pervis never asked him for money to spin his records. He knew if he had gotten involved in any payola, he never would have gained Chess's trust, and ultimately the job. Leonard did not like his folks to take money. He knew it was illegal and that he could lose his license and that they could go to jail. He had been trying to give Pervis money, trying him out to see if he would take it, but he never would take a nickel from anybody, not from

Leonard Chess, the Gordys, the big record labels, no live human being. If someone had said Pervis took money, they were just lying. He never took money from anyone to play a record, and he was proud of it.

"Pervis, come on in. Have a seat, please," Leonard invited as Pervis entered his office.

"As you probably know," Leonard continued, "I've just acquired a radio station, WHFC. I was wondering if you'd come over and do the all night blues show. You know I wouldn't want to fight the blues over at WOPA."

"Hmmm," Pervis said, "if your station is going to be 24 hours, Black; and I'm working on a station now that's just got little bits and pieces of Black programming, I think I'll join you. I think I'll come over to your all Black station, but first I want to know how much you're going to pay me."

They came up with a pay scale, and Leonard Chess told him what he was paying the other disc jockeys.   Since Pervis already had a job, Leonard Chess offered to pay him somewhere in the neighborhood of $250 a week, which was good back then. So, Leonard Chess put him on nights.

Now, this new radio signal would go much further than WOPA's because WVON's (then WHFC) transmitter was centrally located. As far as Black people were concerned, this was the center of the city for a transmitter. WVON has the west side on its right, the south side to the left, and downtown at its back. The signal would cover basically the whole city. At night, it wouldn't get too far into the suburbs, but it would get to Robbins, Harvey, and everything southwest. It would take care of all the places that the Black folks lived. The people in Gary would listen all the time because there wasn't as much interference in the airwaves then as there is now.

E. Rodney Jones was the program director and he was responsible for putting the hand picked staff together. Rodney and he talked, and Pervis said, "listen, I'm promoting shows and I need you to help me put some on."   Rodney was elated to know that Pervis would include him. Pervis knew he had a sure enough job then. He was responsible for all the live shows in Chicago at that time, even before he came to WVON.

The newly formed WVON staff included Pervis Spann the Blues Man,

Pervis Spann

E. Rodney Jones

14

who was on the air from midnight to 5 am. His position was basically the only one that remained in the same spot, because no one really wanted the night shift. He thought some of the disc jockeys would rather quit than work midnights, so he really felt he had job security. Bud Riley, played gospel. He didn't stay at WVON very long. He was replaced by the bishop of the airways, as Pervis used to call him, Bill "Doc" Lee, or William Lee. It was believed Bud Riley had a little run in with some of the management and they let him go after a short span, like a month or two, and replaced him with Bill "Doc" Lee.

People were so amazed that here, on the air, was blues playing all night, then came gospel in the morning, and later on that morning they had rhythm & blues programming. Pervis remembered a lady telling him she thought it was some type of magnificently cruel April fool's joke, resembling a haunting one night stand, magnificent at first, then turning cold-blooded the morning after; but this April 1st event was no joke. Excitement rippled through the Black community, crackling, seeming as if the transmitter of the station was plugged directly into the current of one's soul. Franklin "How Sweet It Is" McCarthy, the sugar daddy, was the music mechanic. Then there was "Rock with Ric," Ric Ricardo, who was at the station temporarily until he was replaced by Ed "Nassau Daddy" Cook, a very funny guy, with the Happy Hour. Also in the mix was, "The Mad Lad" E. Rodney Jones, Al Benson and Herb Kent "The Cool Gent," a great prankster, and now a radio Hall of Famer. Herb said he got his handle, "The Cool Gent" from a school friend of his who, upon his excitement of returning from the army and finding his buddy on WVON, suggested he call himself that, and it stuck.

Part of what made WVON so unique was the fact that it added stimulating conversation with Mr. Wesley South, the Godfather of Black talk radio, hosting "The Hot Line." He soon found out that no matter what you talked about, more often then not there would be someone in the listening audience who knew at least a little bit about the topic, call in and give his view. He would always attempt to keep his beliefs to himself. If there was anything happening in the Black community, you heard it first here. Blacks got the opportunity to hear about political issues, and candidates running for office.

15

Sprinkled throughout the daily programming was the sophisticated and glamorous Bernadine C. Washington with "On the Scene with Bernadine," featuring everything you wanted to know from fabulous fashions to fantastic fantasy. Her mere presence seemed to demand respect. With crafty expertise and a grand sense of style, she was able to speak her mind in a remarkable way as to not offend, but to enlighten. Nobody took affront if she suggested to one of the on air personalities a change of clothing might be in order for an appearance later that evening. She kept all the "Good Guys" together, and was definitely the lady in charge, the matriarch. If she told you something, she had solid logic for it, and was correct 99.9% of the time.

Roy Wood reported WVON News. He was in the same era as Al Benson. Hamms Beer was buying the Roy Wood Show, and he didn't have anywhere to go as the result of his show being sold. Rodney Jones felt Roy was too talented to be out of work, but WVON had a complete staff of people. Rodney decided they needed a news department, and Roy Wood started his news career at WVON. He turned out to be such a dynamic news director. He would give commentary and end it with, "now run and tell dat," and was also famous for saying, "it's enough to make a Negro turn Black." He became known as kind of the authority of WVON's position on things. Air personalities were being jockeyed around so much, until they finally got squared away as to how the line-up would be.

Most of the disc jockeys knew each other, and if they didn't, they knew of each other. In America at that time, there were not many Black radio stations to work for. The Federal Communication Commission (FCC) regulated all the radio stations, controlling what they could and could not do. The FCC was one of the most discriminatory of all the governmental branches that a Black person ever wanted to deal with because it was controlled by congressmen, many from hick towns in Georgia, Alabama, Mississippi, Arkansas, the Carolinas, and places of that nature. They set the rules and regulations radio stations had to follow. This is one of the reasons that kept Blacks from owning any stations. Black folks wanted to work at the radio stations, but they had to go to some white guy, hat in hand, and beg for a job. The FCC had not been a wholesome place for Blacks trying to get into the main stream of radio, television or any

Franklin McCarthy   Bill "Doc" Lee

Ed Cook   Herb Kent

Bernadine C. Washington

Wesley South

Bill Crane

Roy Wood

Lee, Montegue, McCarthy, Spann

Washington, Spann, Lee

communications. To this day, to make sure not too many Black people are involved in the radio industry, they set the prices very high. The FCC did the radio stations basically the way the powers that be did the land in America. When they were quite sure that most of the good land was pretty much gobbled up by the whites, they came out and said, "you Black folks can now have some land." It was usually in the swamps of Mississippi, or the hillsides of Georgia. When the FCC came in, they made sure all licenses of the big class one stations, and even the twos were gone. Then way down the line they said, we're going to allocate a few licenses to the Blacks. These were usually class four stations, which is what WVON was, class four meaning the lowest power that they would give to a community. Back in the early 60s, out of 10,000 radio stations, less than five were owned by Black folks. The class four stations were

250 - 1000 watts. The highest was class one. When it came to Black folks, they raised the prices so high until even if you wanted to own a station, you couldn't. So, Blacks were content, then to have a WVON, and WVON later was content to have two great 'engineers', over time.

The station had its own engineers, an Italian guy by the name of Pat Sarone, the chief, and another one named Walter Childress. Pat was supposed to be a number one engineer, but the 'Good Guys' had their own 'engineer'. It was a 14 year old boy who used to come to WVON and stay with the DJs. He had an office in the back. His name was Larry Langford. This young fellow knew almost as much about electronics as anyone. When he was about 14 or 15 years old, he built a radio station, in his home, up in his attic. His parents didn't know anything about it. The FCC found out and saw this little boy had invented it, and couldn't believe it. They made him cut it off. When there was a technical problem at the station and Sarone couldn't do anything about it, they'd call Larry. Larry was one of the good guys. Later he did the news for WVON.

Years later, they had a disc jockey by the name of Bill "Butterball" Crane. His strong point was that he had a first class engineering license, complete with a Masters Degree. He would know how to come in and take care of a problem he heard on his way to work. Even the chief engineers at the radio station relied on his judgment. This made him invaluable on and off the air. Both he and Larry could make a class four station sound like a class two. With just 1000 watts in the day and 250 watts at night, WVON covered Chicago, basically because of these two electronic geniuses.

It was a marvelous thing, and giving to the community was always a major part of the station's activities. The 'Good Guys', as they were dubbed, were known for their big hearts. They gave out Christmas & Thanksgiving baskets that they collected from different vendors, to the poor and needy every year, donating over 1500 baskets annually. They would don tuxedos and go on stage at DuSable High School, and McCormick Place's Arie Crown Theater, to do the holiday programs that nobody wanted to miss. They would also host charity basketball games. Every year they'd play the Harlem Globetrotters. Tens of thousands of people would come out to see them at the Stadium or International Amphitheater and they would give those proceeds to charity. In true WVON fashion, they gave their all. And the music . . . The music ranged

Jesse Jackson with Marvin Gaye

from Stevie Wonder to The Temptations to Marvin Gaye, just to name a few. It included everybody that had good records. Pervis remembered Maurice White, founder and lead singer of Earth, Wind, & Fire saying what a tremendous contribution WVON made to the public by allowing a variety of our music to be heard, from blues to jazz to R&B, and to the development of new artists on the block. Maurice went on to say it gave him the opportunity to see inside the industry, since the owner of Chess records, which he was affiliated, was also the owner of WVON, making his involvement extend to both sides. He said he was proud to be a part of that movement.

Movement. Pervis pondered for a moment on that word. Usually when one said movement in respect to that era, one usually thought of civil rights, and that's exactly what it was. It was a period of transition, with WVON being the Dr. Martin Luther King Jr. of radio. This reminded him of Rodney Jones talking about all the successful records WVON was responsible for launching, back in the glory days. Alvin Cash had one of the biggest records to ever come out of the Chicago area, 'Twine Time'. Garland Green's, 'Jealous Kind of Fellow', started right here in Chicago, locally produced, locally owned. 'Casanova', by Ruby Andrews, was locally produced, and locally owned. WVON was also instrumental in

22

Eddie Kendricks

spearheading the Motown sound. Chicago was Barry Gordy's mainstay. He would get their records to WVON, hot off the press, before anywhere else, because that would guarantee him hits since WVON was the most popular radio station in the country at that time. Rock and Roll Hall of fame singer Eddie Kendricks, former lead singer of the Temptations, was also part of the Black music empowerment conducted by WVON in the '60s and '70s. Eddie often spoke about how important this station was for R&B artists back in the day. Pervis remembered one particular observation Eddie made that went like this: "WVON made Motown, they made Chess Records, and they made King records, because other DJs wouldn't play Black records on white stations then. As a matter of fact, they wouldn't even let Black people be on the cover of their own albums. They would have two white couples dancing."

Not only were there artists and disc jockeys helping with the movement, but also Black record promoters. A notable one was named Leroy Phillips, who promoted for the RCA label. He used to work with Richard Stamz. WVON played an instrumental part in his promoting Black artists. White disc jockeys didn't want to play Black records, and white program directors wouldn't talk to Black promoters. There was one white promoter by the name of Paul Gallas who was responsible for a lot of Black crossover. Leroy would work with him to get his records played. The first record Leroy promoted was "Everybody Plays a Fool," by The Main Ingredient. WVON played it first. Immediately, record stores Barry's, Fletchers, and Colorite all bought 15,000 copies. Gardners bought 10,000. RCA had never sold that many records so fast. Another one of Leroy's records that took off in sales, thanks to WVON was William DeVaughn's, "Be Thankful For What You've Got." Even though Pervis was the 'Blues Man', every now and then he would play other records. He did that with "Be Thankful For What You've Got." Leroy couldn't get anyone else to play it in Chicago except WVON. When Pervis played it, it caught on, and 65,000 copies were sold in one week. The record company and some radio stations were speechless. This record did that well, and wasn't even on anybody's play list yet. That type thing went on over and over again. A couple of other records that stand out in Pervis' mind that Leroy was responsible for promoting and WVON was responsible for getting them off

24

Leroy Phillips (center) and 21st Century

the ground were "She's Got Papers On Me," by Richard 'Dimples' Field and "Do You Remember the Rain," by 21st Century. With Leroy's promoting skills along with WVON's air play, these records (among others) soared.

Pervis was proud that his station was playing all the hot stuff, and folks were actually ecstatic.

"Knock, knock, knock."

Pervis's reminiscing was interrupted by some rapping on his door.

"Who is it?," he asked.

"James," came the response from the other side of the door.

"Come in."

Pervis knew James Miller and Adolph Peevy had been working on some brick laying on the property earlier and that they had planned to stop by to see him later.

"How's it going?" Pervis asked as they entered his office.

"It's going pretty well. We should have the job completed tomorrow," James said. "What are you doing in here all by your lonesome, Pervis?"

"Well, I was just thinking back on the early days at WVON."

"Those were really some good ol' days, Pervis. I remember them like it was yesterday," James said as he pulled up a chair. He and Adolph had known Pervis for the past 40 years. They were good friends and could talk about just about anything.

"What I remember most about 'VON is the impact it had on Chicago,"

25

James went on to say. "I think it was a wonderful force. We hadn't experienced Black music of that proportion since I was born. Every now and then we might here a Black tune, but when WVON came on the scene, it was like being born again. We had the best DJs, and we had the best music. I bought a '55 Ford convertible in about 1962 or '63, and I put that top down and turned that radio up, and just about everywhere you went, you could hear WVON. Everywhere you'd go, if you went to the beach, if you went down on the lake front, I don't care where you went in Chicago, you were going to hear WVON." James settled back in his chair and Pervis could see the far away look in his eyes.

"I had a friend that owned a record shop I used to work in," James continued. "His name was Mr. Williams, Donald Williams. I worked right next door to the H&H restaurant, which was on 51st Street, and I ran into some of the best people coming out of H&H. They'd leave out of there almost any time, and come into the record shop. That's how I chanced upon you, Pervis. When you came into the shop, we immediately knew you were someone famous because you had the "gift of gab." Then I heard you on the radio station, and my boss told me who you were. I knew then I had met a true celebrity. Yes, that was quite a while ago, but I still remember it. Don't you Adolph? We all go back 40 something years now. As a matter of fact, we belong in the 40 plus club. I can't say enough fantastic things about WVON. Anything I say would have to be amazing, because it was the best thing that ever happened to Chicago."

"If you wanted to hear good music, you should have tuned into WVON," Adolph chimed in, without missing a beat. "My experience, dated back a long time ago, after having met Mr. Spann at an early age, and knowing all the people that he sponsored that was coming up during the, I guess you could say, the good times, in an age that Blacks were really catching on. Pervis, you truly did a lot for them, promoting some of their stores, and promoting them, themselves, such as Ms. Maybelle and some of the other good cooks in the city. You really played a major role in helping Blacks overcome some of the things that blocked them out, you being in the radio community. You came, you hung, and you stayed there until it became a reality. WVON was a household word, and you, Mr. Spann need to be congratulated."

26

"Thank you, Adolph. It's always good to hear another perspective, one from the outside looking in," Pervis replied. James stood and Adolph began to zip his jacket.

"Well, friend, we have to get on out of here. It was good sitting here chewing the fat, but we need to finish up this job early in the morning. I'll give you a call tomorrow after it's over," James said as he made his way to the door.

"So long buddy," Adolph added.

"Good night."

After they'd left, Pervis got up and went down the hall to the studio to begin his midnight blues show. The phone lines were already lit up in anticipation. He couldn't remember a day entering the studio that the phone lines were not lit. Reaching over for a Howlin' Wolf CD, The Blues Man began his broadcast. "Good morning, good morning, good morning. . ."

Hues Corporation, Tyrone Davis, Leroy Phillips

Clinton Gent and the Hues Corporation

Dramatics and Leroy Phillips

O'Jays, Leroy phillips, Clinton Gent

Leroy Philips and Charlie Pride

Teddy Pendergrass and The Whispers

Leroy Phillips, Jim Raggs and Tyrone Davis

Stephanie Mills (center)

Silver Convention, Curtis Mayfield and Leroy Phillips

Pervis Spann

At 5:30 a.m, after rapping up his midnight shift, Pervis got into his car. It never ceased to amaze him how his spinning of the blues all these years still connected with that certain group of the population who let the sultry, hypnotic, and sometimes humorous lyrics of the artists invade their beings and touch the core of their emotions, especially the women.

He chuckled to himself as he remembered the first time he announced on the air that he would not take calls from any men during his show. That was about a month into his broadcast some 40 years ago, but the same thing held true today. He couldn't see the logic in being up all night talking to men, when a soft, sexy voice was much more appealing. As he cruised north on I-55 heading home against the commencement of rush hour traffic, Pervis let his thoughts cruise, once more, to the days when WVON took Chicago, indeed, the nation by storm.

It was about a month into the new era of WVON. What Pervis had thought was going to be just another gig turned out to be a radio phenomenon of epic proportions. He didn't think anyone was really prepared for the major impact of this new station. So, when he announced, during one of his broadcast, that he would not be accepting calls from men, to say he created quite a stir would be putting it mildly.

"Hello, this is the Blues Man. Talk to me baby," Pervis said to one caller shortly after his announcement.

"Man, what's this about you not taking calls from-" click. Pervis hung up on the deep voice at the other end of the line.

There were several reasons why Pervis decided not to talk to men. One was that he wondered why he should talk to a man who's going to be talking about a woman, when he could talk to the woman, herself. Another reason was he felt that some men didn't treat the women right. He didn't like abusive people. Often times he would hear about abuse from men to women. The men were, of course, stronger than women, and the women were, sometimes smarter. A lot of them had dropped out of school, and would carry that title of "man" , and wanted to run everything. Pervis didn't like that and refused to talk to the men because some of them were so abusive to the women. They used to beat up the women and treat them all kinds of ways. He didn't believe a little dainty body of a woman could take all the blows being imposed upon it by a brutal man. So if a man wanted a record played on his show, he would have to have his woman, wife, sister or daughter call, otherwise Pervis wouldn't take a man's request. He had a saying, if you had a man and a job, you need to quit one of them. He just didn't believe a woman should have to work. Pervis knew some men sat home and pretended they couldn't find a job. It had been his concern all the time that women would go out and work, come home and have to cook, be the clean-up person, prepare the children for bed, while at the same time the man was faking. Therefore, that woman had been grossly misused and abused as far as that type of situation was concerned, especially back then. Pervis felt if there were any way he could help punish that man because of this mistreatment of that woman, he was justified. If he could make that man's life a little more miserable than it was, it would serve the purpose. If things got to a point between the couple that it could not be worked out, they should get a divorce. Pervis didn't believe in any man beating up a woman. There is no sense in a woman being married to a man who was going to go up side her head, have her work, then take care of him and the children. He didn't like it then and he doesn't like it now. A few men threatened to go up side Pervis' head since he refused to accept their

37

calls. He would just hang up on them. Of course, none ever did, but it was just the passion WVON created that made everyone want to be a part of it some way.

"Ring . . .Ring . . ." The phone rang again that night long ago in the past.

"You've got the 'Blues Man'," this time a woman's voice was on the other line.

"Mr. Blues Man, can you help me?" the caller asked.

"What's wrong, baby?" inquired Pervis

"My car was stolen. It's a black 1959 Deuce and a Quarter," she said.

"Have you called the police?" asked Pervis.

"Not yet. It has the license plate GJ 2644," she volunteered.

"Okay, I'll announce it during my broadcast, and you be sure to call the police," Pervis finished.

"Thank you Mr. Spann," she then hung up the phone.

It was nothing unusual for people to call the station in times of trouble before they called the police.

"Ring . . . ring . . . ." The phone rang again.

"You've got the 'Blues Man', talk to me," he said.

It was another soft voice. "Mr. Spann, this is Marita, you know you are jammin'. I've got my tape recorder set, but you keep talkin' during the songs and I can't record, and I don't mean just at the beginning. You're talking through the whole tune," she complained.

"Well baby, I guess you're just going to have to go out and buy the record," Pervis quipped, and replaced the receiver.

Before he had gotten off the air that night, he was pleased to know the young lady's car was found. He was flattered to think since he had mentioned the description of the vehicle and the license number several times during his blues show, that he was instrumental in its recovery.

He came back to reality, and let his thoughts return to what James had said earlier about windows being down at the lake. In the summertime you could also hear WVON coming out of certain houses. Folks didn't have air conditioning and a person could hear the music floating from house to house, throughout the community. The station truly wowed the public. Nothing like that had ever been seen before, nor since. That was the make-up of WVON. It was like a great big old loud speaker in the area, just doing its thing with music.

Black folks from all over were so proud of WVON, at least they said they were, and Pervis believed them. Judging by the ratings of the radio station, it was indeed the truth. Any time a 1000 watt station beat out several 50,000 watt stations, the ratings spoke for themselves.

Arriving home and back to the present, Pervis unlocked the door, and went in. He thought he'd grab a bite to eat before he lay down. After 40 plus years of working the night shift, he had developed a routine that involved him catching a few Zs before getting engaged in the days activities. He didn't have to work that night, it being Friday. This is the night Richard Pegue played "The Best Music of Your life," but he still had to go into his office to take care of a little business.

Pervis lay down but couldn't get to sleep. It was like the spirit of the 60's and 70's had come back to live again in the form of his musings of the oh so unforgettable days when WVON had taken a life of its own and invaded every space that beckoned its tantalizing presence, addicting all who came in contact. Again, he allowed the intoxicating memories to take him higher, deeper into the realm of his pschye.

His name was Richard Pegue and the year was 1968. A thought within a thought occurred to Pervis. Isn't it funny how thoughts are things? His chose to revisit the past randomly, not in any sequential order, so he decided to just go with the flow.

Lucky Cordell was responsible for Richard landing his spot on the station. Lucky came aboard around the tail end of 1963 or early '64. He began his career at station WGES back in 1951. He stayed there a couple of years, then went to WGRY in Gary, where he spent six years. After that, he came back to Chicago to WGES where he had his own show. In the old days, any Blacks who worked at WGES worked under the auspicious old 'Swing Master'. It was the Lucky Cordell Show, but an Al Benson Production. Eventually, 'GES was sold and became WYNR. WVON opened and kicked up so tough, that WYNR became all news. Lucky stayed there maybe five months after they went news, because he had always been a music person. That's when he came over to WVON and became one of the 'Good Guys', and soon thereafter, manager, replacing Bob Bell, the last white manager at WVON. Richard Pegue, the only 'Good Guy' besides Pervis still at the station, was one talent put on the air by Lucky.

Actually, Richard first became a fixture at the station in 1965. He was already in the recording end of the business and had a group whose record was being played on WVON. The group was Little Ben and the Cheers, and they had a song called "I'm Not Ready To Settle Down." Richard was their manager; however, he had known Herb Kent for some time. Starting in '66, or '67, he was one of the many guest teen disc jockeys that Herb used to have as host on Saturday evenings from 6:30 to

7, even though he was 24 years old at the time. When the guest DJs didn't show up, Herb would call him at about 6:15, or he'd call Herb, and he'd say, "alright, they didn't show up," and Richard would jump in that green '64 Volkswagen, leave 83rd and Racine where he lived, and be at the station no more than a couple of minutes late. He actually went on the air, sitting in for Herb in 1967. Before going on the air, he was in the sales and merchandising department, then the music director. This led to his involvement in programming. He did the music for the station for about two years, and also dabbled in photography. At a rate of 64 words a minute, Richard also used to type the top 40 play list.

Richard Pegue

By the early 70's, with the unparalleled success of WVON, Pervis was busy outside the station promoting shows and other activities taking him on the road. Somebody had to do his radio broadcast. Since Saturday nights were a busy night for Pervis, he resigned his show on that night, and that is how Richard finally became a permanent on air personality.

Now his record spinning style was different. This is what made WVON so successful. Each DJ had his or her own way of doing things. It was called personality radio. There were no research groups to decide what a certain DJ would play. His ear would be the decision maker. Oh, there was a play list, but the program director, for the most part, let the DJs have a say, accomplishing a uniqueness that set each one apart from the rest.

Herb Kent created an extremely menacing character called "The Gym Shoe Creeper," that he used to weave in and out of his broadcast. He modeled him after a man who lived in Altgeld Gardens who wore very

Herb Kent

funky gym shoes, and never changed them. The "Creeper" would, according to Herb, wait for an exceptionally hot day, 105 degrees or so, then sweatily lay for some unsuspecting woman to walk down the street, knock her down, pull off his gym shoe, hold it to her nose and say, "sniff my sneaker."

His next creepy creation was the "Wahoo Man," who came to being as the result of two beautiful girls, dressed to the nines running in a panic down the street. It turned out this old man was standing in a doorway with a little black dog. He had a terrible face with running sores, an old hat, a long coat, and a broomstick. He had lunged at the girls and they ran. So Herb went into a restaurant and started eating chili and the man came in and started leaning over everybody's table. He leaned over Herb's table, and the man's face was actually dripping in his chili. Herb told the man he had to get out of there, so he left him and went up to the cashier, and the cashier said, "old man, get out of here," and the old man said, "I'll kill you," then turned and left. When Herb walked out, the man was still there, actually singing the blues. As Herb got in his car, the old man, dog, and broomstick followed closely behind. He proceeded to raise his broom stick to start beating Herb's car. This was the year old Cadillac Herb just purchased, his first one. It was a pre-owned car by Muhammed Ali, complete with fist print in dashboard. It was a cool automobile with an

41

alarm and switch, and Herb had a particular fondness for it. He only had it for about a week, so as the man raised his stick to strike the hog, Herb quickly flipped the alarm switch, and the old man started chanting with the siren, "Wahoo, Wahoo. Wahoo don't scare nobody," and he ran down the alley. So the guy, now in the penitentiary, had been known as the "Wahoo Man" every since.

Since Richard often stood in for Herb, and sometimes Pervis, he had to be an original. He did not try to copy anybody's style, especially Pervis', because everybody knew there was just one "Blues Man." Of course, when he used to sit in for Pervis, he would play the blues because it was Pervis' show and that is what was played at that particular time. But when the show became his, Richard played the dusties, old hit records.

He remembered the day Richard officially started. The radio station was having a promotion, and cars were packed in the parking lot. Everybody was coming to get their free WVON transistor radios, that only picked up one station, WVON. It caused a major traffic jam, and the state police were out there on Kedzie directing traffic. Of course everybody was in place at the station. So to Richard, it all seemed like "wow, I'm in 'big time' radio." Although he knew some of the people already, to be employed by them was a different thing, different in terms of he'd heard it and seen it, and now he was part of it.

Richard also had his own 'mascot' for his broadcast. It was something called a 'dubber ruckie', which is rubber duckie backwards. He had a little squeeze toy that made a sound, and every now and then he would squeeze it. Listeners used to approach him and ask about his dubber ruckie. He even had a huge following at the Cook County Jail. Richard became aware of this when a nasty situation was about to break out at one of his public appearances, and two former inmates stepped in to shield him from any unpleasantness. He received mounds of mail from them, and played most of their requests.

When WVON first hit the air waves, Richard's response was the same as everyone else's, even though he was heavily into the music business at the time. That same contagious excitement got him caught up because here was a station with all "us." Before WVON, there was only integrated radio. Blacks were fortunate to have some spots, but not all. A person couldn't wake up anytime and just turn on the radio and have guaranteed Black music, until WVON. Richard was overwhelmed just like the rest of the population. Back when it all began, Richard was working in a major record shop in the city, so he was already in the industry, but from that side. It was all beginning to come together for him. By him being in retail record sales, going to a radio station was somewhat of a natural progression. Yes, Lucky Cordell was responsible for Richard landing his spot at the station. This was Pervis' last lucid thought before drifting off into a deep dreamless sleep.

Temptations, Al Green and E. Rodney Jones

E. Rodney Jones, Diana Ross, Billy D. Williams

He woke up, refreshed and ready for the day. Then showered, dressed, and headed to his office.

As Pervis drove north on Kedzie, he prepared to turn into the WVON parking lot. It was about 2:00 in the afternoon. He looked around the lot and noticed it was full. They were promoting all types of events for the WVON 40th year anniversary that would take place throughout the year. There were calls to make and dates to line up. As he parked the black van with the blue WVON logo, he glanced at his other car parked in the lot. He noticed some guys by the car and tried to make out the identity of the individuals. Just as he adjusted his neck to get a better look, he saw his 1950 Chevy start up and begin to exit the lot

By reflex action, Pervis threw the gear of the van he was in into drive and started to follow his car. As it peeled on to the street, burning rubber at the light, Pervis realized his automobile was being stolen. He immediately stepped on the gas and began the chase in earnest. The abducted vehicle sped South on Kedzie and turned left at 39th Street. As luck would have it, the light turned red when Pervis approached. With dismay, he saw his car disappear out of sight.

Pervis let out a disappointing sigh, and turned around to go back to the station to call the police. After he phoned them, he sat down and waited. Of all his years of working at this same spot, this had never happened. He worked nights and would be so involved in his music, anybody could have had the chance to steal his ride. Why today, on this bright and sunny afternoon? He stopped asking why and thanked God he happened to be arriving at the time his car was leaving.

"Ring." The sound of the telephone interrupted his thoughts and he picked it up.

"Hello?"

"Hello, is this WVON?" asked the caller.

"Yes."

"Do you have a 1950 Chevy, with a WVON 1 license plate?"

"Yes."

"Your car is parked in my lot. Two Mexican guys pulled up and got out the car then jumped in another car with a white guy and another Mexican in it and sped off."

"Where are you located?" Pervis asked as he grabbed his keys. After getting the exact address, he left to retrieve his stolen vehicle.

After securing his car with the now peeled steering wheel column safely in his private lot in the back of the studio, Pervis began making arrangements for the up coming 40th year anniversary celebration. He was always into promotions, in fact, he had been promoting artists long before his days at WVON. Pervis again went back down memory lane.

His first office when he was a promoter was in The Southmore Hotel on Stony Island. He had a secretary, who was about 15 years old, named Minnie Ripperton. She would always go down to Chess Studios and sing background for artists like the Dells and Earth, Wind, & Fire. She had a voice that was unbelievable. If Leonard Chess was recording Etta James and he needed a back-up singer, Minnie Ripperton was one of the people he would use. She was the first secretary Pervis had who knew anything about the business. He, himself, was fresh in the business. He had a record store at 1350 E. 64th St., where Minnie worked part-time. Everyday after school, Minnie would come by. When she left his office, she would go down to Leonard Chess' studio. Pervis soon blossomed

47

B.B. King

around all those big named entertainers to be, though he didn't know it at the time. He was still at WOPA and most of his time was spent outside the office selling accounts for his blues show. His success on the air was determined by how many accounts he sold. He'd bring the accounts back to his office, and Minnie would type them up.

While at WOPA, he began to promote. Around that same time, he and Big Bill Hill partnered to promote a show featuring B.B. King. It was a big show. That show came about due to the fact that somewhere down the line, B.B. King had a run in with Big Bill Hill. Big Bill Hill was basically the only other one in Chicago who would really play a B.B.King record, because at that time, the blues were essentially classified as country. B.B. King would sing it and Big Bill Hill would play it, that is until their disagreement. It turned out, he and B.B. King were looking at the same woman, so, they were a little angry with one another. Since Big Bill Hill would no longer play his music, that left only one other blues man in town, Pervis. Both men were older than Pervis, and generally their women were too, so they didn't have to worry about him looking at them, besides he was only looking at one woman, his wife, Lovie, since he was a newly wed at that time.

Pervis kept playing his B.B. King records, and B.B. wanted to come to town. Now Pervis had been promoting smaller blues acts with artists like Magic Sam, and GL Crockett, because B.B. King was the creme de la creme of blues singers. A step up from those fellows to the likes of B.B. King was a bit intimidating. Pervis felt he didn't have the charisma, ability or know how. So he talked with Big Bill Hill one day and told him he had a deal with B.B. King. The only thing Bill didn't realize was that Pervis had never put on a show of that caliber. Pervis didn't realize, then, that there was a rift between Bill and B.B.. Big Bill Hill said "I don't touch him. I don't play his records and I don't want to be bothered with him."

"This is my show," Pervis said, "if you want to participate, I'll split the profits with you."

"You will?" Bill asked.

So this made them partners. Pervis, a novice at putting on shows, went out and got the biggest place he could find, The Ashland Auditorium, which was located on the corner of Ashland and Van buren on the west side of Chicago. Other than that, he basically followed Bill's lead, to see how everything would work. After they went through that phase of the business, Pervis knew how to put on a big show.

B.B. King was ripe for Chicago because he hadn't been there in several years since he talked to the wrong woman. He was the hottest act going because he hadn't been in Chicago for quite a while. Big Bill Hill wouldn't play him and no one else was putting on any grand shows but Big Bill Hill. Then Pervis came in and started putting them on. He put on this show in conjunction with Big Bill Hill because he wanted to see what all he had to do to put on a show of that caliber.

Pervis paid the rent at the Ashland Auditorium and they said he could use the bar. Bill Hill dropped his argument with B.B. King, and that night they had a sell out crowd. The place could hold 3000 people; but, they ended up with about 3500. Some of the people never really got all the way upstairs. There were so many trying to get in that some had to stand on the stairs just to see B.B. King. Pervis had never seen any thing like it. It was a huge crowd, truly amazing. People where everywhere. The show was a colossal success. As far as Pervis was concerned, he saw more money than ever before, and during that time, times were hard. It took until about ten or eleven o'clock the next morning to count all the money. It was more money than Pervis had ever seen in all his life. He never counted that much money before, coming from the steel mill, radio disc jockey school, and going to school to be an electronic engineer. He never had a real need to count that much money. Here now, they had thousands of dollars, most in little bills that had to be counted. After he got to about $300 or $400, his eyes began to get tired. The next day Pervis got up and went looking for a house. After that, Big Bill Hill wanted to be his partner again.

Their succeeding show was Little Junior Parker. He had a hot hit record called 'Driving Wheel'. That show wasn't as successful as B.B. King's show. They had it at the same place with about the same amount of liquor. It started snowing approximately two days before the show. By the time the performance hit the stage, there was about 12 inches of snow on the ground, which disrupted the entertainment. Big Bill Hill was running the bar, drinking, and Pervis ran the place. When Pervis got ready for the money to pay Junior Parker, Big Bill Hill had sneaked out the back door with it. So Pervis had to pay Junior Parker the next day with some of the money he made from the B.B. King show. This broke up his friendship and partnership with Big Bill Hill. Pervis never did get the money back from Bill. He said he was drunk, but he obviously knew what he was doing. This resulted in E. Rodney Jones becoming Pervis' new partner when he came over to WVON.

After WVON had got going very well, Pervis solidified his affiliation at the Regal Theater, and began to produce shows there. He had put so much pressure on the Regal Theater at 47th and King Dr. when he was at WOPA that the guy over there by the name of Mr. Brant was keeping his eye on him. Brant was a Jewish individual and wanted to know how he could get a little money from some of the shows that Pervis was producing. When Pervis came in, he told him, "well, I have no problem in cutting you in on a little money, but I want to make sure I make some money, enough to cut you in on." He only had to make sure Pervis got all the dates that he wanted, and he did. He saw that Pervis got everything that he wanted. Pervis took care of him, too. They took care of each other. They had a mutual admiration, money, and the older Mr. Brant was working for the corporation that was running the Regal Theater at that time.

By Pervis working all night, he was in the best position to do many things throughout the day, with just a few hours of sleep. He could see the ball games in the day and the fights early evenings, then lay down about 9:30 or 10:00 to take a little nap, get up and get right back to the radio station to do his midnight broadcast. It was all very convenient because he lived 20 minutes away.

Life was good, and things were going well for Pervis. He had a safety valve at the Regal Theater with the manager, a Mr. Brant. He had a complete friend and a safety valve at WVON by the name of E. Rodney Jones. He had a safety valve with the owner of WVON because Chess knew that Pervis Spann was considered a very honorable, trust worthy individual and he was not going to do anything to jeopardize the license of the radio station; therefore, things were beginning to fall in place for Pervis Spann and WVON. Within a few months after the opening of the radio station, Pervis and Rodney gave their first concert at the Regal featuring Stevie Wonder.

It was the first time Pervis met Stevie Wonder. He was a little boy staying at The Roberts Motel. Pervis was taken in to see "Little Stevie Wonder" and remembered thinking, "why, he's just a growing boy." A person could look at him and tell he was going to be a big guy. They introduced him to Pervis, and he asked Stevie, "what are you doing?" Stevie answered and said, "I'm watching T.V." Pervis looked at him kind of strange because he wondered how a blind person could be watching T.V. Then Stevie said, as if reading his mind, "oh yea, I understand what's going on." By the sounds, he interprets just what is going on on television. Pervis found out from some of Stevie's managers that he does it consistently at home.

The Stevie Wonder concert ran, at the Regal Theater, for seven days. It was very successful. That was the performance Stevie Wonder made the 'Fingertips' album.

When artists announced they were coming to town, WVON would push their records real hard, and folks would buy them, making that artists real popular. After the stars arrived in town to put on their concerts, the performances would draw a huge audience because people would come out to see those particular artists that were popular. Yes, everything was just about squared away. Promoting shows and having WVON went hand in hand. REP Productions (Pervis and Rodney) would put on some of the best concerts in town because they had a hot radio station, sparkling, really going. When they knew a star was coming to town, they'd play his records, and the advertisement was instant. It was one of those deals where you couldn't miss. It was just that simple, a magnificent marriage between radio station WVON disc jockeys and the Regal Theater.

Stevie Wonder

Spann, Lee and Jones

B.B. King, Muddy Waters and Alvin Cash

Pervis put his thoughts on hold once more and began thumbing through his rolodex. He was going to call some of the 'Good Guys' to see if any of them would be available to participate in the 40th year anniversary celebration.

He thought he'd begin with Don Cornelius. Don was really the first one to guest star for him when he was promoting on the road. Don's rich resonant baritone always had a deep impact on the listening radio audience.

"Hello, may I speak to Mr. Cornelius?"

"Who shall I say is calling?"

"Pervis Spann."

"One moment please."

"Hello?"

"Hey man, this is Spann . . ."

What was supposed to have been a quick call inquiring about Don attending the 40th year anniversary festivities turned out to be a conversation going over events of the past 40 years. They talked about getting licensing approval from the FCC, to the early days at WVON.

"Hey Don," Pervis said, "every time I go home in this weather, like what we've been having, the one thing I really always think of is the night you and I left here and you were driving me home. We were going down to the express way, the Dan Ryan, in your Oldsmobile, and you had no heat. It was cold, about ten below."

They both laughed and went on to talk about the Soul Train music awards Don just produced, and how he was the one true success story coming out of WVON.

"Tell me what to tell my girls. They said on the fifth of next month, they want you here. Can you come? Melody is the President out here now at WVON and my other daughter, whom you've probably never met, Latrice, 27 years old, is the vice president, so the Spann's are in charge." After a brief pause, "okay, then, get back to me," Pervis said to Don when he said he would see if he could make it from Los Angeles.

He lay the phone gently in its cradle and remembered how Don Cornelius began his broadcast career at WVON. He was first a Chicago police officer who also sold insurance. One day, Roy Wood committed a traffic violation and was pulled over by Don. As Don approached his vehicle, Roy presented his license and Don asked all the questions police usually do when a person is stopped. This caused Roy to comment on Don's voice. He told him that he was in the wrong profession and that he needed to come by WVON and see him and do an audition tape. So Don took him up on his offer, and that is how he began his broadcast career at WVON radio.

At first Don used to answer the telephone for Wesley South, during his popular talk show, 'Hotline'. He then began filling in for the guys and sometimes did the news, but once he started hosting a local dance show called 'Soul Train', Leonard wanted to terminate him; however, he left voluntarily. He went on to take his local show to Los Angeles, where it became a tremendous success, and is still popular today. Don Cornelius and Herb Kent were responsible for most of the practical jokes around the station.

"Excuse me," a voice interrupted Pervis reflection. "Are you busy?" A head peeped around the half closed door.

"George! Great to see you," Pervis answered as he got up to greet his friend. He and George O'Hare go way back. "Sit down."

"I came here with Dick Gregory. He's in there with Cliff now. I just

George O'Hare, Pervis Spann, friend and Mayor Harold Washington

thought I'd visit with you awhile. How's it going?" George asked, pulling up a chair.

"It's going," responded Pervis as he headed for the sofa. "I just finished talking to Don Cornelius, trying to see if he could make it to the 40th year celebration. Are you coming?" he asked George.

"Wouldn't miss it. That's funny you would be talking to Don. How's he doing?"

"He's doing great, just busy," Pervis said.

"I remember when I first met Don. It was right here at WVON. I didn't know who he was." George began. "It was during the time I was the merchandise and sales manager at Sears Roebuck and Co. I had the appliances and the televisions, but I also had the record department, and I found out that was my love in life because the record department

58

brought me to a lot of parties. Every night, there was a new record. Weather it was Barbara Striesand, Aretha Franklin, or whomever it might have been, I was out there every night, getting free records by the way, and all I could eat and drink. I met a lot of wonderful people in that business, of course from the different radio stations in the city and the record companies. I was also part of the volunteers of the Southern Christian Leadership Conference- Operation Breadbasket, when Dr. Martin Luther King came to town. The ministers, of course surrounded King, in the early days and they had meetings on the south side. They'd plan the picketing and different things like that. That was prior to Jesse Jackson coming on board. One day I had the opportunity to drive Dr. Martin Luther King here, to WVON radio. At that time, I really didn't know much about WVON. I knew that it was a radio station, but remember, I was white, and I was advertising records at all the white stations, or lets say the white newspapers, until I got direction from Dick Gregory on how to do it. Anyway, I went to the station with King and of course I walk in and I realize I don't know anybody there and King, was of course, the greatest. He was going into the Wesley South Hotline show, and I turned around to leave. There was this gentleman sitting on a milk crate outside the studio. He said, "Who are you?" I said my name's George O'hare. He said, "What do you do? Are you working with Dr. King?" and I said no, no. I just happened to drive him over because it was a ministers meeting and I just did that. He says, "oh, so you have nothing to do with him?" and I said no. "What do you do?" I said, well I'm the advertising manager at Sears Roebuck and Company for appliances and records - "Oh" he said, "why don't we go out and have a drink." Well, we went out that night and had a drink at Flukeys. I think it was at Flukeys or the Tiger Lounge, but all I know is that one had a two o'clock license and one had a four o'clock license and I didn't get home 'til five a.m. Don had a dream that he was going to have a television show. He didn't tell me the name of the show. The first reaction I had, not knowing him, I didn't want to say at the time. I knew that Nat King Cole, who was the greatest singer of all time, you might say, could not keep himself on television because the southern white TV stations wouldn't put him on because the advertisers didn't want it and he lost his show. Well then time went on and finally I

Don Cornelieus and Pervis Spann

did say to Don Cornelius, this is ridiculous. You're not going to get a show because you're not going to keep a show. It's just not going to work. I said, Nat King Cole could not do it. How could you do it? Who are you? That was my attitude towards him, and ah, he came in with his wife about two years later and said he'd like to do this, and I said to Delores and Don, this is not going to work, and we went and had a drink. Then we started double dating with my wife and his wife. We were doing the old lobbying and then finally, Wesley South and Don Cornelius came to my office at Sears State Street store, where our group office was, and they said they got this idea about this program, this television show, and I saw it down as 'Soul Train'. What's a 'Soul Train'? I wondered. That made no sense whatsoever, but I did call the national record buyer. I did that because I do not, as a record advertiser, get any money out of my pocket for Sears. It had to come from the record companies to be delivered to the radio stations or the newspapers to advertise the records. So I said, we don't advertise rhythm and blues, first of all, and the idea of advertising on 'Soul Train' doesn't make any sense 'cause I'd have to take money out of my budget for that. So I put him on the phone with Dick Mabbet, and Dick Mabbet talked to him. He was the national record buyer, and he said "look, it's the same way at the national, we take money only from the record companies and spend it with the newspapers and the radio stations. We just don't do that the way you want." So we decided to go and have a drink. We started to walk toward the elevators and the phone rang. It was my secretary saying, "Mr. Mabbet would like to talk to you and Mr. Cornelius." It was like God working in mysterious ways. Motown called at that moment and said they wanted to do something soulful in Chicago. I'll never forget when Don got on the telephone with Dick Mabbet. Mabbet asked him, "what is soul?" And Don said, "well, soul is soul, you know what I mean? It's soul, soul, you know soul, soul." Mabett went on, "what's a train got to do with it?" "I don't know," Don said, "we call it Soul Train." Well, with that, Dick Mabbet said, "let's do it." I think the price was $100 a day, for three commercials on Channel 26, which was the lowest rated station in Chicago at that time. So, I was thinking this is ridiculous to go on that station. I told that to Don, even though we agreed to do it. The contract was set for 13 weeks, $100 a day, five days a week, but I tell you Don, I said to him, it's not going to work. Let's go have a drink. So we went out to have a drink, and I kept telling him, this station's not going to do it. Well, Don went out and put on the first show, and it was a monster. That second show, a monster, the next show, a monster. And as a result of that, when I would go out at night with Don, to the different bars or different parking lots to park the cars, prior to that show, no one had said anything to us; but, as soon as the first two or three or five days of that show, all of a sudden they're going, "S -o-u-l- T-r-a-i-n," everybody's saying, "S-o-u-l T-r-a-i-n" because they see Don Cornelius, and his presence caused that to happen. And it caused me to believe the unbelievable. A little station like that could garner that much popularity; but, see we did not know, as white advertisers, the market. We always thought Black folks, of course in those days we said "Negro" folks had no money. They were unemployed. They were poor. As a result, we didn't go after that market whatsoever. And if it weren't for Dick Gregory telling me about the market . . . Like he asked one day, "where do you advertise?" I said Columbia records gives me money, and I put it in the Chicago Tribune. He went on to ask, "what kind of records do you have?" I told him, and he said, "those are rock-n-roll records. People that buy rock-n-roll records don't read the Tribune." The best of all was one day Dick Gregory said to me, "I understand you got a new job." I said yea, and he said, "you're the record manager for Sears," and I said yea. He said, "records. That's the 45 rpms and albums?" I said yea. He said, "now you've been to your 63rd and Halsted street store. What did you see?" I said I saw a beautiful display of Elvis Presley. Dick Gregory said, "Elvis who?" I said, Mr. Gregory, Elvis Presely. He said, "who's he?" I said, come on. He said, "no, no, it's Sam Cooke." I said, who's he? He said, "Sam Cooke is the star." I asked, what do I do? "Get rid of the display of Elvis Presely and put a Sam Cooke display up." So I went back to the office then and I said, there's no Sam Cooke. I don't have Sam Cooke in my listings. I told Greg. He said, "that's the problem. You got to get Sam Cooke." I asked, how do I do that. He said, "just tell your record company, you want to get Sam Cooke." I told my record company, which is an all white record company, and they said, "no. We don't have Sam Cooke." So I called Greg back and he said, "go and see Ernie Leaner." I went to Ernie Leaner. I got the Sam Cooke. We put the records in the store, and the biggest mistake we made is that we forgot that the 79th street store was there, and the Gary Indiana store was there. We had put them all in Englewood, and advertised to the total Chicago area, and the people around 79th street and in Gary almost had riots because there were no records."

"I remember Sears advertising on WVON. How did that come about?" Pervis asked.

"Again, I have to lay the credit at Dick Gregory's door. He gave me the advice as to how to advertise to the Black market. My people at Sears didn't know how to spell Black at that time. They didn't have any love whatsoever for the Negro market. So, as naive as I was, I came to the office early one day, and called my advertising agency, McCann Ericcson, and I said Jack, I'v got a new gig we're going to do. We're going to put these commercials on, there going to be 30 seconds and 60 seconds on WLS, WVON--he stopped me short and said "George, we can't do this. You can't put them on WVON." I asked, why not, and he said, "it's run by a bunch of ex-convicts. They're communists." So I said to myself, oh God, I'm going down the drain at Sears. So I didn't say anything back to him. I got off the phone and called Dick Gregory, and he said, "George, George, George, I think you know we've been lied on for so long. That's a lie. Do you know, George O'Hare, that the FCC runs the radio stations. You have to be a better citizen than anybody else to conduct a radio station because of the fact you have to be clean." I asked him what was I going to do? And he asked me, "who's that guy you introduced me to at one of the Sears functions about a month ago?" I told him it was Gar Ingraham, and he suggested I go to him for advice. So I went to Gar, I said I couldn't believe this is what McCann Ericcson said. He called them all communist and all ex-convicts. Gar said, "are you serious? Go back to your office and wait for a call." I go back to my office and about 10 minutes later, the phone rang. It was an apologetically laughing Jack from the ad agency. "George, ha, ha, ha, I think I probably made a little mistake. Of course we'll put them on WVON." That's what was going on then, unlike today where racism is more subtle."

"One good thing came out of it. It brought you to us," said Pervis.

"WVON was so powerful then. That brings to mind another incident," George went on. "In 1965, I got a call from Dick Gregory and he said, "you got to go to WVON. You're going to see something you're not going to believe." So I came down here. Mahalia Jackson was here, and everybody that was anybody politically Black was in this building. I think I was sitting over there where Deacon Wayne sits, the little place he has now where you can see through the glass. The whole subject was tomorrow there would be no school. Tomorrow, they urged, stay home. They're going to boycott the Chicago Public Schools, and I'm sitting there asking myself, is this the right thing to do? I was a novice in the civil rights movement, and I was scared. I saw this and I thought, this is the

Herb Kent (far right)

craziest thing in the world. Why would mothers and fathers not bring their kids to school? You just don't do that. See, I didn't know the fever, the fever of the movement at that time, and the next morning, the kids didn't go to school, and the next morning they didn't go to school, and the next and the next. Then all of a sudden I saw in the newspaper that somebody made the comment that the schools in Chicago, and all over the country get federal funds based upon attendance. The whole boycott was based on the board calling themselves trying to solve the integration problem for the white folks by putting wagons around the schools. They called them 'Wllis wagons', named after the school superintendent, Ben Willis, designed to keep the Black folks in their area, and the white folks could be free from having Black folks come to close to them. That's what the trailers were for that they put outside. Because of the lack of funding, all

64

of a sudden everybody started saying, "well I guess we better get rid of those wagons," and they did."

"Beep." The intercom in Pervis' office signaled the voice of Cliff Kelley. "Spann, is George O'Hare back there?"

"Yes he is."

"Ask him to step around here, Greg wants to ask him something."

After George O'Hare left, Pervis went back to work, seeing which of the other 'Good Guys' would be available for the anniversary celebration.

He decided he'd contact Herb Kent next. Of course, Herb was the one who introduced Leonard Chess to Mr.Hoffman and got the ball rolling for the acquisition of WVON, since Herb already worked at WHFC, the station's call letters before being bought by Chess.

As they talked, a startling thought struck Pervis.

"Herb, do you remember when Leonard Chess got beat up?"

"No, when?"

"It was around the time he bought WVON."

"I remember when a guy took a knife to him," Herb said.

"No, not that. I mean really beat up. He was walking around looking really bad, all battered and bruised, with a cut above his half closed eye." responded Pervis.

"Who in the world beat him, the mob?" Herb asked, intrigued.

"It appears so," Pervis answered.

"I know he was tight with Nat Turnerpole, and Hymmie Weiss who had that record label, 'Old Town'. Arthur Prysock was on it after a while, and a couple of du wop groups. Hymmie Weiss was a big mobster, but his father was a 'real' big mobster. They were Jewish guys, Jewish mobsters. I don't remember when Leonard got beat up, though," Herb said.

"Well he did. He got the hell beat out of him," Pervis added.

"That's the record business for you," said Herb.

"Yep, yep, yep," Pervis agreed.

"Oh, do you know who should come? Did you call his brother Phil? He was one gentleman we never had a cross word with, a real nice guy, just the opposite of his brother Leonard. Not that Leonard was a bad guy. He was more of a fiery hands on guy, and Phil was always in the background with the balance. I think he'd love to come," said Herb.

"Yes, Phil was always fair. Do you have his number?" Pervis asked him.

"I don't have it. He's in Tuscon, Arizona, though, on a ranch. Ah . . .you know who could get to him? His son. If you could get hold to him. He was at the "Loop." Didn't they own the "Loop?" Herb asked.

"The "Loop" what?" asked Pervis

"The "Loop" broadcasting, WLUP. They used to be part of that. That boy, what was his name?"

"Marshall?"

"No, not Marshall. Marshall Chess is Leonard's son. He's in New York, I think. You could probably find Marshall if you call BMI, because he's got to be getting some of those residuals, and Marshall could get you to Phil. I know he'd love to come."

"I'll keep that in mind, but we can count on you Herb?"

"I'll be there, and on time. Hey Spann, do you remember when we were hosting that event at McCormick Place, I forget what the event was, we did so many there. But this particular time, I was a little bit late, I had the tendency to run a little late those days. Everybody was waiting for me, and in tuxedos. I brought mine, and it was curtain time. All the 'Good Guys' helped me put that tuxedo on. It was amazing to feel all those hands on me." Herb laughed. "Another time that stands out in my mind is around 1970. Joe the pilot hosted the WVON champagne flight on the lake front, out of the now defunct Meigs Field, and Jay Johnson, one of Joe's flight students, was the co-pilot that day."

"Well, you know the 'Good Guys' could do some of everything. Who else was there?" asked Pervis.

"Cecil Hale, and Richard Pegue, I know for sure. We had a very nice time. We'd take off out of Meigs' Field, fly around Chicago, and come back and land. It was called a champagne flight because there was a brother with a cooler in the back with champagne in it. The Electric Crazy People were there. I asked Joe to loop that plane and he said we'd die if he did that."

Pervis chuckled and rang off. Herb continued to linger in his mind. He was one of the wildest of the 'Good Guys'. By wild, Pervis meant outrageous, but in a humorous way. He remembered one time when Herb was at the Regal Theater with him, and Herb had a man in a casket. That man, of course turned out the be the Wahoo Man. They had about 2500 people at the Regal, and the man came out the casket. This created quite a stir.

In the mid 60's, Herb also was instrumental in popularizing two types of men's fashion, the 'Ghouster' and the 'Ivy Leaguer'. He took that Ghouster/Ivy League battle and made it one of the biggest things in the city. The Ghouster jacket was the signature piece for that look, usually worn with baggy pants and pointed toe shoes, and the Ivy League was more of the Brooks Brother suit, penny loafer type. 'Cherry' the tailor was the guy who made the Ghouster jackets. He had a location on 63rd and Cottage, and did very, very well, mainly thanks to Herb. Herb would pit groups of one style up against the other and listeners would call in and tell what category they'd fit in. Ladies would also weigh in with their preferences so that the friendly rivalry extended to the high school "record hops" Herb hosted regularly. He also had a comedy act called 'The Electric Crazy People', who would perform on his broadcast. They covered the Spaniels' original record, "Good Night Sweetheart," but changed it to "Good Night Herb Kent." This used to be his official sign off record for a time at the station.

In addition to being humorous, Herb was a humanitarian. Along with sponsoring the Ghousters vs. the Ivy Leaguers, The Electric Crazy People, the Wahoo Man, and the Gym Shoe Creeper, Herb did his part in the civil rights movement. Not only was he the MC when Dr. Martin Luther King Jr. gave his great speech at Soldiers Field, but he (along with the other DJs) was credited for quelling the riots after King's assassination. He got on the air at WVON and encouraged listeners to get off the streets and stop the fighting. He dedicated a portion of his show everyday to students, insisting they stay in school. Yes, Herb was a jack of all trades. He didn't mind taking a nip every now and then, either.

Pervis never drank or smoke, even though he was co-owner of one of the hottest clubs in the city, the Burning Spear. He remembered when he bought the Burning Spear, a night club on Chicago's south side.

Pervis got up from his desk and walked over to the couch to get more comfortable. Just those two conversations he had with Don and Herb took him, once again, on that sentimental journey through time, to an era when he felt he could do anything, and often times did.

Talking to Don earlier about his car with no heat reminded him of that snow storm in 1967. He'll never forget it. Pervis arrived at work that night. He didn't even try to pull into the parking lot. That was impossible. Nobody made it in the next day. The manager at that time, a Lloyd Webb, had to helicopter in. Lloyd didn't stay long, because he was back on the helicopter when it flew back out. Pervis had to end up staying there twenty-four hours to help keep the station on the air. It ended up something like 27 inches of snow. Yes, in those days, Pervis was equal to any challenge presented, or at least it seemed.

He remembered when he first saw the spot to become the Burning Spear. It was the old Club Delisa, and it was for sale. At first Pervis wanted it to be a skating rink (which he eventually got) but his new partner, E. Rodney Jones and his business manager Verlene Blackburn out voted him, and club it was. This was around the same time he landed his position at WVON. The Burning Spear was located at 55th and State. Rumor had it that it was owned by the Mafia. This rumor proved to be true, but Pervis didn't know it at the time. He and Rodney went into it together. It was in pretty good condition. He had a few carpenters around to help, and whatever wasn't in place, got put in place. The lighting was stupendous, the best Pervis had seen up until that time. He thought the person who wired it must have had great vision and knew it was going to stay around for a long time. Since it had been previously owned by the wealthy Delisa family, they had the best craftsmanship a person could have hoped for. After tightening up all the minor cracks and leaks in the roof, it was good to go. Now all they needed was a liquor license, which was not hard to get since it was a club and zoned for liquor. There was an alderman by the name of Kenneth Campbell who had a guy working for him by the name of Cliff Kelley. Kelley was a

70

Washington and Redd Foxx at the Burning Spear

young democrat and helped Pervis secure his license, once he complied with the city's requirements. Since Pervis was never a drinker, he basically handled the business side. Before they opened up, he didn't know what to buy, so he left that up to Verlene. She bought thousands and thousands of dollars worth of liquor, because down in the basement, there was a great big old cooler. The cooler would hold 150 cases of beer.

Once everything got set, in early 1964 they opened the doors. There was a very nominal cover charge, five dollars. Maybe once or twice they'd take it up to eight dollars. If a thousand people showed up, and considering liquor sales, they didn't do too badly per night. With everybody in their finery, there were no fights. It was an integrated spot with a pretty elite clientele. The Beetles came by one night and sat in with the band, and so did Elton John. The atmosphere was nice and mellow. The city even had a bus, like casinos do nowadays, that would pick people up and drop them off at the club.

The stage was a masterpiece. When a show was over, the stage would come down about eight inches from the floor, and all the folks who wanted to dance had a dance floor. When they got ready for the next show, the stage would go back to the designated position. They had comedians as well as musicians take center stage, such as Redd Foxx, who performed there many times, so did Sonny and Pepper, Dick Gregory, Godfrey Cambridge and others, many of the same artist who used to be on Wesley South's talk program.

They had everything going that people would ever want in a club. It was successful right off the bat, from day one, just like WVON. Promoting artists, hosting concerts, and spinning records all went together like a fine tuned machine. There was an artist who came along by the name of Al Green. WVON really played a huge part in building his career. Pervis and Rodney had him so hot, it was extraordinary. By this city being so big, other markets would find out what records WVON was playing through various rating companies such as Billboard, then they'd get right on it and play it and help make it a big hit in their markets, too. If a DJ was in Jackson, Mississippi and heard from some promotion man that a record was hot in Chicago, he'd immediately play it. Soon it would

72

be number one there, too. This happened across the country. The same thing happened with REP Productions. Due to their success at the Regal Theater and The Burning Spear, Pervis and Rodney put on concerts everywhere, from Madison Square Garden in New York City, to shows in Detroit, Michigan, Cleveland, and Dayton, Ohio. It didn't matter. If an entertainer was hot here, odds are he'd be hot in some of the other markets.

Rodney Jones and Pervis Spann worked for WVON, ran the Regal Theater, and owned The Burning Spear. Leonard Chess was making so much money with WVON, he didn't have time to worry about what his DJs were doing in the Black community. Herb Kent was doing the teenage hops in more than one place, and Jones and Spann were doing night clubs. There was a place called the Treanon Ballroom. It would hold 5000 people. A typical week went something like this: WVON would play records of Jackie Wilson, Bobby "Blue" Bland, The Miracles, and Marvin Gaye, in heavy rotation, along with the regular programming. On air personalities would announce these same artists' upcoming appearances daily. Then on Friday night, it was show time. They would have Jackie Wilson at the Treanon, Bobby 'Blue' Bland at a place called "The Packing House" on 48th and Wabash, and they'd have the Miracles and Marvin Gaye at The Regal. The Regal would be over at around nine o'clock pm, then the people would go on down to the Treanon, and after that, the Burning Spear.

When it came to Black people, WVON and REP Productions had the town all sold up as far as entertainment was concerned. The shows needed the station and the station needed the shows. WVON was so popular, that if you heard it on WVON, it was the truth. If you wanted some entertainment, it was coming through that same radio station.

A buzzing from the intercom snapped Pervis back to reality.

"There's a call on line two Mr. Spann. It's Ms. Blackburn."

"Thank you Denise. Hello?"

"How ya doing Spann? It's Verlene."

"Hi Verlene. You would not believe what I was sitting up here doing. I was thinking back on the good old days when we had The Burning Spear popping."

"You must have a good memory. You know I suffer from CRN?"

Verlene Blackburn and Mrs. E. Rodney jones

"CRN? What's that?" asked Pervis

"Can't remember nothin'. But listen, Spann, I have to stop by there.
You know I'm on the 40th year anniversary of WVON committee and I
have to go over a few things with Melody. I was hoping to stop in and see
you. I'll be there in about an hour."

All this reminiscing seemed to make Pervis sleepy, so he decided to
take a power nap right there on the sofa until Verelene showed up.

♫ ♫ ♫

Driving on I-94 heading south, Verlene Blackburn wondered why in the
world Pervis was thinking back on those days, although those were some
of the best times of their lives, she had to admit. With this 40th year
anniversary celebration coming up, she guessed it was only natural to
look back. She permitted her thoughts to drift back, back to when she,

Burning Spear Nightclub

Spann, and Rodney were a team. Spann and Rodney were the owners of the Burning Spear and she was the manager.

Actually, she didn't set out to be a manager. She knew Spann because she was married to his wife's brother, and of course had known him and Rodney from the radio. In fact, she and Spann go back way before his radio days. She remembered when he used to spin records at a show lounge called Earl Collins Bar-B-Que. He was spinning records, driving a cab, repairing radios, and working at the steel mill all at the same time. He was always very busy, doing something. She believed he became interested in the entertainment business as a result of his spinning records at the lounge.

She never will forget when WVON first hit the airwaves. Each disc jockey was unique. She remembered Spann hanging up on the men who

75

phoned, Ed "Nauseau Daddy" Cook calling the Dan Ryan express way the Damn Ryan and Rodney, with that oh, so melodious voice! WVON was all you heard. There was no other radio station in Chicago. It was "the" station and just a great time was had by all.

A great time was also had at the Burning Spear. Verlene was the first Black woman in Chicago to manage a nightclub. It was nothing she set out to do. It all started when Spann and Big Bill Hill put on a show on the Westside at a place called The Ashland Auditorium. BB King was the performer. Verlene had gone just to see the performance. She saw all the people at the door and how the cashier was handling everything. She found Spann and asked him if he took a starting number so they would know how many people paid to get in, and he said no. When she went inside, she wanted to know if they had taken inventory of the alcohol, but no one had. So she just stepped in, and sort of took control. She smiled remembering when it was all over. Spann had never seen that much money before. She just started counting. It was daylight when they finished. They were actually counting money until ten or eleven o'clock the next morning. Because of her quick thinking, and take charge mentality, Verlene became the manager of the Burning Spear.

The opening night of the Burning Spear was just as exciting. She'll always remember the gorgeous gown she'd purchased for the occasion. It was black velvet with a deep V in the back, and a split worthy of a double take, very flattering to her small but statuesque 5'2 physique. She had silver sandals, stockings and jewelry. She knew she wouldn't need a purse because she'd be on duty. Unlike the night at the Ashland, Verlene came prepared to work. She, Spann, and Rodney, were all very excited. She had never seen so many people in her life. The line went from 55th and State, around the corner all the way down Michigan Ave., and Spann got so nervous.

"We've got to open the doors, we've got to open the doors, we've got to open the doors," he kept repeating.

"But the doors are not supposed to be opened yet. We still have things to do," she answered.

They opened the doors anyway. Rodney and Spann were walking around in their tuxedos, with their chest all poked out, and Verlene was walking around with rollers in her hair, and no shoes on, complete with sweat pants, looking like a lost child. She actually thinks people thought she was the housekeeper. She never did get a chance to wear her beautiful gown. Despite all that, they had a very successful opening night.

Verlene returned to the present as she returned to the historic WVON studios. Its been a while since she worked there. Four years, to be exact. After 17 years of working at the "new" WVON, she felt it was time to step aside. She entered and was immediately shown to Melody's office.

Wilson Pickett and Walter Jackson

Duke Ellington

Herb Kent, Charles Knox, LaBelle, E. Rodney Jones

Gene Chandler, Lovie Spann, Pervis Spann, James Bevel and B.B. King

Irv Kupcinet, Jesse Jackson, Lena Horne

Janet Jackson

Ray Charles

Pervis woke, startled. He felt his ears burning as if someone was talking about him. Glancing at his watch, he noticed about an hour had gone by. He sat up and readied himself for Verlene's visit. They had a great relationship. She'd been with him from day one at the Burning Spear, and later at WVON.

He knew he was blessed to have had a Verlene Blackburn. She could do everything! Every since she and one of her crooked partners, by the name of E. Rodney Jones, out voted him on whether the new building should be a skating rink or a club, and it was proven that they had a better view point and insight on what could happen, Pervis couldn't hide his appreciation. By him being directly from the country and never having been involved in anything like night club ownership, he really didn't know what was going on. He now brags about the fact that Verlene was one of the people that was in the corporation where they had the Burning Spear. Actually, the corporation was not supposed to be the Burning Spear. It was technically, supposed to be his skating rink. But, in the American Way, he went along with the ones who won that particular election.

Verlene felt strongly there was a need for a club in Chicago in the '60s. A niche needed to be filled.

There were no chorus girls and floor shows. In fact, she always said, . . .

"Excuse me, am I interrupting?," came a smooth voice from the doorway. She strutted in as she presented the question. They always had a good working relationship and their rapport proved it.

"Verlene, it's good to see you again." As they embraced, Pervis helped her with her coat and presented her with a seat.

"Believe it or not, I was just thinking about the time you said we needed a club to fill a void and since I was booking shows, you felt I could bring in the talent," Pervis said.

"Which you did. I vaguely remember the decor of the Burning Spear when we first entered the premises; however, we did a complete overhaul. Remember the beautiful cocktail lounge we had in the front where people could have drinks while waiting to go into the main room for the floor shows? And how about our 'Devils' the waitresses who were hand-picked by me?" Verlene couldn't seem to stem the flow of memories that invaded her being since earlier this evening.

"How many waitresses did you have working there?" asked Pervis.

"I believe maybe 15 or 23, with the head waitress, Willie White."

"That was her name?"

"Um hum. Playboy had the 'Bunnies' and we had the 'Devils'. We had some of the prettiest Black girls in Chicago, or on the face of the earth. We had them from high yellow to pleasingly, pleasingly, plum Black. They were all fine, and they wore red uniforms with a devil's tail and horns, which were also picked and made by me. Before opening night we had, I don't recall the lady's name, but she trained the Playboy Bunnies, do you remember that?"

"Yea, I remember that."

"And she came in and trained our girls on how to be a waitress, or how to be a devil," she finished. "I was just remembering how long that line was opening night."

"Yea, the Burning Spear-"

"It really wasn't called the Burning Spear yet," Verelene interrupted. "We called it 'Lisa', but the Delisa family didn't want that. We couldn't use their name legally, but we weren't using their name anyway. We were calling it Lisa. Then we changed the name to the White House, and that name didn't go over too well. From there, I think you came up with the name the Burning Spear."

"No. I came up with the name 'Club'."

"Oh, the Club, right, the Club. And opening night, I remember it was McKinley Mitchell and Johnny Williams, both gone to soul heaven. I remember when it was time for them to pick out their dressing room downstairs, and each one wanted the star dressing room. I don't recall who actually got it. Then we had the Julian Swing Dancers, our chorus girls. We had that hydraulic stage."

"How many chorus girls were there?" Pervis wanted to know.

"I don't remember, but we had quite a few. Some of them are still living here in Chicago, and one of them has her own dance troop. The only other thing I remember about opening night is that it was super packed. No one else had floor shows and chorus girls in Chicago then. We were the only ones in the city doing chorus girls. We had all of the top entertainers of the time, up and coming. You know you introduced a lot of the stars, well, today's stars. We're talking 40 years ago. You know I was still in high school," Verlene added with a wink. "However, I do recall Rodney Jones bringing in Wayne Newton."

"There were a lot of folks that came in, not as an artist to perform, they just came by and performed while they were there, like the Rolling Stones," said Pervis.

"Also, Spann, a lot of important people attended. We had many of the social clubs, prominent social clubs having their affairs there."

Silence filled the room, as if they both traveled back, in their own mental time capsules, each embracing different encounters.

Pervis was first to break the quiet.

"It was another world in show business."

"It's where we both received our comeuppance," Verlene added.

"You all wouldn't let me drink, so I never really had a reason to want a social club," Pervis said.

"But you had a ball, didn't you?" Verlene reminded him, and burst out laughing.

"Yea, I did," Pervis admitted with a smile.

"And you also did your radio blues show from there," Verlene mentioned.

" Um hum. What other entertainers can you remember performing there?" Pervis asked

"I remember Roy Hamilton. He passed away shortly after his performance," Verlene said.

"Roy Hamilton was the creme of the crop when it came to entertaining," Pervis added. "Whenever Roy Hamilton finished his show and went back to his home, I would always get a letter thanking me for booking him. His voice was almost unbelievably good. He used to sing 'Ebb Tide', and so many others. I would have to look them up. Do you remember any of his tunes?" Pervis went on to question.

Verlene answered and said, "No, but I know 'Ebb Tide' was everybody's favorite. Then we had Joe Williams."

"Joe Williams was more or less from Chicago. He hooked up with Count Basie somewhere, but he made periodic appearances for us down at the Club. We had so many of them. T-bone Walker performed there. Red Saunders often came by. Before we took over, he was the house band there for 20 years," Pervis said.

"Lou Rawls used to stop in, and of course BB King and Bobby 'Blue' Bland. They were regulars," said Verlene

"Do you remember that time we did that benefit for Jr. Parker when he was sick? We took in thousands of dollars, and gave him all the money. We had another show there, where we crowned Rodney Jones the King of all disc jockeys. Pop Staples of the Staple Singers was in attendance."

"Didn't you crown Aretha Franklin "Queen of Soul" there?", Verlene interrupted.

"I did that at the Regal Theatre," Pervis answered.

"I know she became "Queen of Soul" because of you," she said.

"I crowned her on the stage at the Regal Theater, and every since that day she's been known as the "Queen of Soul," recalled Pervis. "She is, without a doubt, the greatest singer of all time. It's my opinion, that there is no greater female voice on the scene than that of Aretha. The charisma, the quality, the beauty, and the sound is unmatched. When I crowned Aretha, I could have just as well crowned her the queen of

B.B. King and Bobby "Blue" Bland

gospel, or just plain queen of singers, not necessarily just the queen of soul; Black, white, brown, or any other color singer."

"How did you first get involved with Aretha Franklin?" Verlene wanted to know.

"I first started listening to Aretha when she was about 16 years old. I used to listen to her when I was back stage. By me being kind of naive, I didn't say too much to her, because to me, it looked like she was underage. When I did finally get enough nerve to say something to her, I'll never forget it. It was at the Regal Theater. I was back stage. Remember how the Regal had those thick, plush, red velvet curtains? Well, I peeped out from behind those curtains and I was feeling good that day. Aretha was singing, and she was really getting her grove on. I looked at her over there on the piano, and I said, 'oh sing it baby, sing it baby'! She sang, 'I ain't never had a man to love me like you do.' And I

Spann crowning Franklin at the Regal Theatre

said, 'sing for me, baby. Sing to me,' and looked up and I was looking dead in her daddy's eyes."

"Then what did you do, Spann?" Verlene inquired.

"I turned away and walked off a little, and I turned around and looked, and he was still glaring at me," Pervis laughed. "I knew I had done something wrong to Rev. Franklin's daughter, and I don't think he appreciated it."

A few moments of silence filled the room before Pervis continued.

"After Rev. Franklin gave me that ol' 'you better watch yourself' eye, I figured that I'd better do just that. Aretha Franklin was singing so good, and she sounded so marvelous carrying those notes so far, and high, and low, that I don't think even Aretha knew how wonderful she sounded, especially to a man, a young man like me at that time. When she walked on the stage, every man in the Regal Theater stood and all the women

89

Spann crowning Franklin Queen of Soul (courtesy of Jet Magazine)

Johnny Taylor

Albert King

were so proud. When I put that crown on Aretha Franklin's head, Red Saunders, the maestro there came on the stage along with E. Rodney Jones. We just had an exceptional time. That was one of the high points of my career at the Regal Theater, putting that crown on the queen's head. You don't know how good it made me feel to put that crown on the queen's head, a sho 'nuff queen."

"Is that the only place you had Aretha, at the Regal?" asked Verlene.

"No. When I was doing a lot of shows on the road, I used to play Aretha in many, many places. I played her in Dayton, Ohio, and we had sell out houses on every date we played there. I played Aretha in St. Louis, Missouri on more than one occasion. I played her there several times with Johnny Taylor and Albert King. One of the big ones we played Aretha at, other than Chicago, was Atlanta, Georgia. We went there and played at a place called the Omni Arena. It held 18,000 people, and we had it packed out. It had one of those great sound systems, and it was distributing a sound so beautiful, it was like a different world. Some of my fondest memories of show business were when we had Aretha on that tour. We went to several other places, and let me tell you, I had a lot of female singers, I mean a bunch of female singers, but none, at that point could equal an Aretha Franklin. She did deserve to be, and in my opinion, still is the queen of all singers all over the world."

"And do you remember when you used to have your talent shows, Pervis?" Verlene asked.

"How could I forget?"

" The Jackson 5 . . .," her voice trailed off and she became thoughtful. Then suddenly she burst out, "Look at me. I've gone from can't remember nothin' to CRA, can remember a lot. You've got me sitting here like this. I must get home. I'll see you at the WVON 40th Anniversary celebration at the DuSable Museum," Verlene said as she made a motion to rise.

"You'll see me next week if you'd like to," said Pervis. "WTTW, Channel 11 is doing a special on the 'Good Guys' of WVON. They've invited Herb Kent, Lucky Cordell, Wesley South and yours truly to be on Chicago Tonight. I'll let you know as to the time and day."

"You do that," Verelene said as she embraced her friend and took her leave.

Melody Spann

Bernadine Washington

Isabel Joseph Johnson

Thirty minutes later, Pervis was in the WVON van, driving south, on his way home. He was glad he had a chance to talk to Verlene. He hadn't seen her in a long time. She had always been his right hand. He knew she was someone he could depend on. Women have always played an integral

94

part at WVON, and continue to do so now. His daughter Melody, is the President, and many women are on staff now, from the news director, to the producers, not to mention on air personalities. Yes, women have and continue to be very important at the station.

Of course, they had Bernadine from the start, who ended up becoming the first Black female executive at a radio station. Back then, it was unheard of to have a Black woman as the Vice-president of a station. To this day the industry remains dominated by men, but in the '70's, after Bernadine worked her way up, she broke new ground, something WVON was famous for. Each thing WVON was responsible for is amazing in itself, but to put them all together was mind boggling, even to Pervis. He knew he was blessed to have been a part of that particular Black History in the making.

"Thank God for Jesus," Pervis heard himself say aloud. He continued to cruise and continued his thoughts

Bernadine also had the 'Bern Club'. The chic way she represented herself was one of the ways she let people know she and the station had class. Part of the WVON frenzy was to be affiliated with the station in some way, and this ultimately led to the development of her club. One thousand Chicago women did charitable work, traveled, exchanged ideas and style. They used to meet at Carrie's Chateau on E. 75th, where they'd learn how to walk, how a lady got in and out of a car, and other socially enhancing skills in a lady like manner. Ms. Washington was supreme elegance. She touched the women listeners in a way no 'Good Guy' could, and the men loved her. Leonard Chess was one of her biggest admirers, and Bernadine, being the good business women she was, knew how to work it to her advantage. Yes, Bernadine was very clever. She knew even back then, women were the true power. Her glamorous sophistication took her a long way in radio. Pervis was almost sure she used her feminine wiles to get her way, but he wasn't mad at her. One couldn't help but respect and admire Ms. Washington.

They also had Isabel Joseph Johnson, who hosted the gospel show, 'Rock of Ages'. Another great voice was that of Yvonne Daniels. She did most of her work on the FM side, but as women became more accepted in the industry, she was able to use her connection to WVON as a spring board in her career.

Pervis sprang back to the here and now, parked the van in his garage, and went inside the house. He sat down, took off his shoes and picked up the T.V. remote control. He was still on the all night blues man schedule. The TV came on already on Channel 11. 'Chicago Tonight' was just coming on. This reminded him of his coming interview with host Bob Sirott. He, Herb, Lucky, and Wesley, back together again. Actually, he and Wesley South never left. Both were major shareholders at the station, with Pervis being majority. He walked over to the refrigerator and took out a half gallon of neapolitan ice cream. Pervis liked it because of its variety, something he could always appreciate. He got a couple of nice scoops and sat back down in front of the tube, then looked at his bowl and made a mental note to walk and extra lap tomorrow when he took his customary exercise at the Dan Ryan Woods. With the volume turned down, he was able to let his thoughts wonder.

It seemed odd to Pervis that he and Wesley would end up owning the station together. Of all the 'Good Guys', these two were the most unlikely pair. He remembered when they first met. Actually, they didn't do too much interacting, with him doing blues on the midnight shift, and Wesley hosting a talk show earlier. There was a song Herb Kent always played when he was signing off, right before Wesley got on, and everybody thought it was his theme song, but in actuality it was Herb's, even though it was quite apropos for the upcoming talk show. The song was called 'Open Thine Eyes'. Pervis knew 'Hotline' was some talk show. He'd had to do more than work nights to not have heard about 'Hotline', Wesley's one hour broadcast, especially, May 12, 1963, the night Medgar Evers was murdered. Wesley had just interviewed Evers the previous Friday before his death. He announced on the air the following Tuesday that he was going to replay it, this time with Evers' widow. So many calls came in to 'Hotline', 50,000 plus, to be exact, that the telephone circuits became jammed and Illinois Bell had to ultimately invent the '591' exchange, still in use today, for radio only.

some of the artists

WVON

helped make

famous

THE GOOD GUYS "SOUL 45" SURVEY LIST

THE BLACK GIANT IN CHICAGOLAND AT 1450

LUCKY CORDELL

BERNADINE C. WASHINGTON

E. RODNEY JONES

ROY WOOD

JOE COBB

BILL CRANE

JAY JOHNSON

RICHARD PEGUE

BILL "DOC" LEE

PERVIS SPANN

HERB KENT

CECIL HALE

WESLEY SOUTH

ISABEL J. JOHNSON

ED COOK

JIM MOLONEY

EARL LAW

JUNE 2---JUNE 9, 1972

1.	I'LL TAKE YOU THERE	STAPLE SINGERS
2.	OH GIRL	CHI-LITES
3.	LEAN ON ME	BILL WITHERS
4.	WOMAN'S GOT TO HAVE IT	BOBBY WOMACK
5.	THERE IT IS	JAMES BROWN
6.	LOOK WHAT YOU'VE DONE FOR ME	AL GREEN
7-A.	JUST AS LONG AS YOU NEED ME	INDEPENDENTS
7-B.	OUTA SPACE	BILLY PRESTON
8.	WALKING IN THE RAIN	LOVE UNLIMITED
9-A.	EVERYTHING GOOD IS BAD	100 PROOF
9-B.	CAVE MAN	JIMMY CASTOR
10.	YOU'RE THE MAN	MARVIN GAYE
11.	I'VE BEEN LONELY FOR SO LONG	FREDERICK KNIGHT
12.	ASK ME WHAT YOU WANT	MILLIE JACKSON
13.	AIN'T THAT LOVING YOU....ISSAC HAYES	& DAVID PORTER
14.	....I DON'T WANT TO BE RIGHT	LUTHER INGRAM
15.	I WANNA BE WHERE YOU ARE	MICHAEL JACKSON
16.	DOIN' MY OWN THING	JOHNNY TAYLOR
17.	I CAN'T BELIEVE I ATE THE WHOLE THING/	E. RODNEY JONES
18.	I ONLY HAVE EYES FOR YOU	JERRY BUTLER
19.	SUPERWOMAN	STEVIE WONDER
20.	THAT'S THE WAY IT'S GOT TO BE	SOUL GENERATION
21.	ALL THE KINGS HORSES	ARETHA FRANKLIN
22.	WE'VE COME TOO FAR TO END IT NOW	MIRACLES
23.	DREAMING OUT OF SEASON	MONTCLAIRS
24.	RIP OFF	LAURA LEE
25.	BEFORE THE HONEYMOON	LITTLE MILTON
26.	THE COUNTRY GIRL RETURNS	LUCILLE SPANN
27.	IN MY WORLD	BRENDA' LEE EAGER & PEACHES
28.	THUNDERMAMA	THUNDERMAMA
29.	I NEED YOUR LOVE SO BAD	JESSIE JAMES
30.	HIGHER & HIGHER	DORTHY MORRISON
31.	IN THE GHETTO	CANDI STATON
32.	I'M THE ONE WHO LOVES YOU	PAT & PAM
33.	IT'S THE SAME OLD LOVE	COURTSHIP
34.	MY LOVE IS COMING DOWN	RUBY ANDREWS
35.	BABY I'M FOR REAL	ESTHER PHILLIPS
36.	KATIE PEARL	LITTLE BEAVER
37.	IS IT YOU GIRL	BETTY WRIGHT
38.	BETWEEN THE LINES	CHARLES WHITEHEAD
39.	BED & BOARD	BARBARA MASON
40.	I ONLY MEANT TO WET MY FEET	WHISPERS

INSTRUMENTALS

1. STORIES--THE CHAKACHAS/2. FOLLOW THE WIND--MIDNIGHT MOVERS
3. GOTTA BE FUNKY--MONK HIGGINS/4. PUT IT WHERE YOU WANT IT--
CRUSADERS/5. MUSIC IS THE MESSAGE--KOOL & GANG/6---SOULTRAIN
A. RAMRODS-B. RIMSHOTS/7. SLIPPIN' INTO DARKNESS--RAMSEY LEWIS

Jackie Wilson

The Miracles

Joe Tex

Bobby "Blue" Bland

Harlod Melvin and the Blue Notes

Little Milton

The Isley Brothers

Peaches and Herb

Roy Ayers with Lionel Hampton

Pigmeat Markham

The Soul Children

Shirley Brown

Otis Clay

Latimore

Al Green

The Dells

Betty Wright

Smokey Robinson

Denise Lasalle

Artie "Blues Boy" White

Jerry Butler

The Chi-Lites

Donald Byrd

The Fatback Band

Clarence Carter

Kool and the Gang

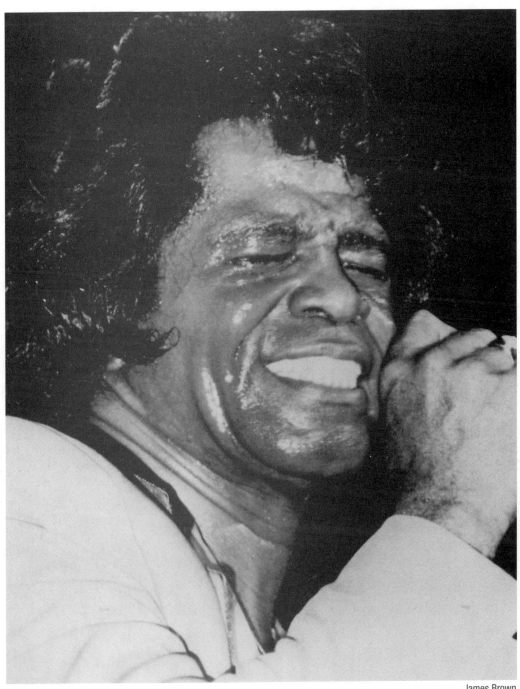

James Brown

Chuck Jackson

Martha Reeves and the Vandells

The Sylvers

Emotions

Nancy Wilson

Natalie Cole

Stylistics

David Ruffin

Rufus Thomas

Curtis Mayfield and the Impressions

Jr. Walker and the All-Stars

Percy Sledge

Barry White

Gene 'The Duke of Earl" Chandler

Z.Z. Hill

Getting Ready	The Temptations
I'm A Blues Man	Z. Z. Hill
Got To Be Some Changes Made	Albert King
Got To Be There	Jackson 5
Love Hangover	Diana Ross
Kiss & Say Good-Buy	Manhattans
Living For The Weekend	O'Jays
Mom's Apple Pie	Tyrone Davis
Let's Stay Together	Al Green
Any Day Now	Chuck Jackson
Midnight Hour	Wilson Pickett
Cold Sweat	James Brown
End of Rainbow	McKinnley Mitchell
The Town I'm Living In	McKinnley Mitchell
Whang, Dang, Doodle	Ko Ko Taylor
Bump and Grind	Z. Z. Hill
My Love Has No End	Nancy Wilson
How Many More Years	Howlin' Wolfe
Young, Gifted, and Black	Nina Simone
Hole In The Wall	Mel Waiter
Blues is Alright	Lil' Milton
Be Ever Wonderful	Ted Taylor
Work Out	Jackie Wilson
Ebb Tide	Roy Hamilton
Ain't Nobody Here But Us Chicks	Louis Jordan
Sitting On The Dock Of The Bay	Otis Redding
Black Knight	Charles Brown
Man's World	James Brown
Grand Pa Can't Fly No Kite	Clarence Carter
Heaven Must Have Sent You	B. B. King

So Good	Tyrone Davis
Little Blue Bird	Little Milton
Twistin' The Night Away	Sam Cooke
Kiss And Say Good-Bye	Manhattans
Woman To Woman	Shirley Brown
Cheaper To Keep Her	Johnny Taylor
Nothing You Can Do	Bobby Bland
Call Me	Aretha Franklin
Getting What I Want	Peggy Scott
Harry Hippie	Bobby Womack
Two Steps From The Blues	Bobby Bland
Shot Gun	Junior Walker
Damn Right	Buddy Guy
What I Say	Ray Charles
Let's Straighten It Out	Latimore
This Time Gone For Good	Bobby Bland
Five Long Years	Muddy Waters
Don't Mess Up A Good Thing	Chuck Strong
Minnie Mae	Marvin Cease
Breakin' Up Somebody's Home	Artie White
Something's Mighty Wrong	Tyrone Davis
Misty Blue	Dorothy More
That's The Way Love Is	Bobby Bland
Bill	Peggy Scott
Chicken Head	Jimmy Lewis
Sue	Bobby Rush
Call On Me	Bobby Bland
Born Under A Bad Sign	Al King
Good Love	Johnnie Taylor
Frankie & Johnnie	Sam Cooke
Big Payback	James Brown
Who's Making Love	Johnnie Taylor

Not only was WVON an outlet for music expression, but to express ones feelings vocally as well. Some of the interviews Wesley featured were with Malcolm X, Muhammad Ali, Minister Louis Farakhan, Roy Wilkins, Whitney Young, Jackie Robinson, Jimmy Carter, Dick Gregory, Robert Kennedy, Duke Ellington and Dr. Martin Luther King, just to name a few. Body guards often had to be on duty to protect the guest from the listening audience. They mostly wanted autographs, but it was just so many. Dr. King preached on non-violence, leadership, and adequate teaching.

A quote from Dr. King during one of his non-violent appearance went like this:

> "People who listen to non violent teaching
> generally respond very well. If somebody preaches
> violence, and seeks to lead people down the path
> of violence, they can also get a following. So, ah,
> I think it's that. I think a Ghandi for instance
> can lead people to high levels of non-violence,
> I think a Hitler can lead people to low levels of
> violence. So it largely depends on leadership, and
> people will respond to non-violence if it is
> adequately taught and gotten over to them that non-
> violence doesn't mean sitting down doing nothing.
> It is not the method of the weak man. It is the ultimate
> method of the strong man. I would be the first to say
> that cowardliness is worst, ah to my mind, than
> violence, and I would much rather see an individual
> standing up against injustice and not being a coward,
> than anything else. But I do think one can stand up
> non-violently, as we've done in so many instances . . ."

Another time Wesley had him on his show was to help combat the housing segregation in Chicago. One of the worst buildings was found on the west side. It was roach and rat infested, dilapidated, everything a person could think of was wrong. Mayor Richard J. Daley cleaned that place up, and had it when Dr. King was here looking like a five-star hotel. Wesley joked that they needed to have King come to Chicago once a week, so that they could re-hab the entire city that way. Dr. King was living here with his family, and Wesley called to invite him on his show. That's how he first got him on. He came and was on for an hour. When King arrived at the studio, there were about three or four people there wanting to meet him. When the show was over and he left, there had to be over 1000 people in the parking lot, and about six or seven police cars. When Dr. King came out, everybody cheered. In the WVON parking lot,

99

there were some flower beds two feet high. A couple of police officers put King up on one of them, and they shined the spot light from their police cars on him. He spoke for about four or five minutes and it all ran smoothly.

Wesley got the idea for 'Hotline' by talking on the telephone to someone at home and thought people should be able to do this type of dialogue on the air. So he presented the idea to Mr. Hoffman, then owner of WHFC before it

Wesley and Dr. King

became WVON, but he couldn't see it. Wesley felt music and talk were not mutually exclusive. Due to the fact that Wesley was a well known columnist for the Chicago American, the Tribune's afternoon paper, and as a result would meet so many people, he felt they should be able to talk with each other, and it would be great because so many people had so much to say. When Hoffman finally sold the station to the Chess brothers, Wesley stayed on them. A 'no' turned into a 'maybe'. Because of Wesley's popularity, persistence, and journalism experience from having worked at Ebony Magazine five years, the Chicago American, the Chicago Defender and his own magazine (until it ran out of money), Chess finally said okay, they'll give him from 11 until midnight. That became one of the hot time spots of WVON. He had about a dozen interviews with the honorable Elijah Muhammad. For security reasons, he never visited the WVON studio. The one he had with Malcolm X after he was ousted from the Nation and just a few months before he was assassinated was very powerful. Malcolm made some cryptic remarks about Muhammad. That was the beauty of 'Hotline'. It was uncensored and the guest could say what they wanted to get out to the public, and the public ate it up.

After the Chess brothers sold WVON, Pervis remembered Wesley recounting this story. Phil Chess, the youngest of the two brothers had

Carl Wright

Spann

very little to do with the station, until after Leonard died. They sold the station in 1970 for $9 million. All the employees put together didn't make $1 million a year. Wesley said he was only making $155 a week, and the others were making around $30,000 a year. Even back then that was horrible. As good as Leonard was, he didn't pay much. Wesley wrote a letter to Phil and Leonard's widow. He told them that they had made $9 million, and that the 'Good Guys' were underpaid, but made this station one of the biggest things around. Yes, they got the glory, but the Chess brothers had gotten all the money. He suggested they take a million dollars and split it among all the 'Good Guys', but he never heard from them. Wesley saw him again some time later. Chess had an office down on Michigan Ave. right across from the Tribune Tower. Wesley could see Phil, and Phil saw him, but turned and went in the back. Wesley always believed if Leonard had lived, he would have given them all something substantial, because when he had run for office for Congress in 1968, Leonard gave him $10,000 plus all the advertising he needed. Phil, however wanted him to repay all the money he had gotten. To Wesley, they were as different as night and day.

Pervis finished watching television, and decided to lie down and try to get some sleep.

♫ ♫ ♫

The next couple of days went by pretty routinely. Pervis did his usual three mile half walk half jog at the Dan Ryan Woods, had lunch with his youngest daughter Chante, a lawyer, taped his television show 'Blues and More', with longtime friend and movie star, Carl Wright and of course hosted his 40 year old all night blues show on WVON. Tomorrow was the live broadcast on WTTW Channel 11 in Chicago. Pervis was looking forward to seeing Lucky, Herb and Wesley again.   He made a note to call Verlene and remind her to check it out.   He picked up his CDs and headed down the hall to the studio to start his show.

Pervis woke the next day and started getting ready for his morning jog. Once he got his routine going everyday, he hated to miss it. He had been on a nice roll lately with his exercise and it felt great.

He arrived at the park, stepped out of the van, and started a light jog.

It was a beautiful morning, unusually warm for early April. He liked to use this time to free his mind. Purposefully, he pushed the recently invasive thoughts of 'The Black Giant', the alias WVON was known by back in the day, from his mind and attempted to clear it of all conscious thought.

Four hours later, Pervis sat in his office, feeling refreshed and confident. Completing his work-out usually gave him a sense of accomplishment, setting the stage for the rest of the day. He picked up the telephone and dialed Verlene's number. After several rings, her voicemail picked up. He left the time Chicago Tonight was airing, hung up the phone and turned on his computer. He thought he'd get some work done until it was time to head out to Channel 11.

As he sat in the WTTW television studio, he and three other 'Good Guys' waited for moderator Phil Ponce to finish interviewing the newly elected city officials so that radio veteran Bob Sirott could talk to them. He still looked good. Bob used to be on in the '70s on a very popular rock station, WLS in Chicago, and had a long career in journalism every since. First radio, now TV. All the 'Good Guys' still look good too. Herb Kent wore his customary cowboy hat, Lucky and Wesley sat looking distinguished in shirt, tie and suit, and Pervis, also suited up was wearing shades.

He heard Bob giving the introduction, telling how Herb used to do his show live from a different Chicago High School every Friday night, and how Pervis once stayed on the air 87 hours doing something called "the sleepless sit in." He went on to introduce the former general manager of WVON, the Baron of Bounce, Lucky Cordell, and the host of the old WVON nightly call in show that brought listeners and national leaders together, Wesley South.

As the interview progressed, Pervis thought he and Lucky needed to hook up. He had just talked to Herb, and he and Wesley see each other from time to time to handle radio business, but he hardly talked to Lucky. He looked over at his old boss and listened to what he was saying.

"We had one of the closest knit family of radio people you'd find anywhere in the country. We loved each other. We were brothers and sisters. We see each other on occasion now and it's always like in the old days. We don't hang out as much as we used to, but we're able to keep

Jackson and Cordell

in touch," Lucky responded when asked by Bob if they had a close relationship in their working days.

They talked about the lack of Black music on the air before WVON, and the acquisition of the station by the Chess brothers, the results of Leonard having come to Herb, and he setting up the luncheon meeting between Chess and Congressman Hoffman, the then owner of WVON (WHFC).

After showing an old picture of Jesse Jackson and Lucky Cordell together, Bob remarked to the people who were not aware of the kind of impact the station had back then, on how the leaders came to WVON.

"We were most receptive. We appreciated Jesse Jackson's message," said Lucky. He went on to say WVON, quite possibly did more than any other entity to build Rev. Jackson and Operation PUSH.

Bob talked to Wesley about his classic interviews and how Roy Wood gave commentary, all this on a music station. They also discussed the 'Good Guys' basketball team, of which Bob presented a picture, and spoke of the days when Pervis managed talent.

"As far as the Jackson 5 is concerned, I heard Diana Ross discovered them. Just like you discovered the moon," Pervis quipped as the group broke out in laughter.

"I managed BB King. I'm the one who put the crown on BB King. I made BB King the King of Blues," said Pervis.

The interview lasted about 20 minutes. They covered 'The Bern Club', Don Cornelius, how he made commercials, and how the station was a lot more than just music.

"You were the boss Lucky, for a while. Did you ever have any run-ins with these gentleman who are acting so civilized now?" Bob asked.

"Well you know what Bob, this is a true story. We never had a problem

'Good Guys' Basketball

between the on-air personalities and management. There was some conflict between ownership, but no. I'm glad you mentioned this. In the WVON play being run, they felt, I suppose, they had to have some drama so they added in to the show that Herb Kent and I had some problem. Totally untrue. Herb is one of my oldest friends. The reason it concerns me is that this was unique and rare for that many radio personalities to get along as well as we did. So, it's kind of like a record I don't want spoiled by giving the wrong impression."

They ended the interview talking about Herb's Electric Crazy People. After Bob Sirott thanked the 'Good Guys' for being on Chicago Tonight, for all the thousands of Chicagoans who don't get to talk to them but who grew up with them, for their contributions to Chicago broadcasting and for making Chicago a better city due to their influences on popular culture and the lives of their fans that continue to this day. They all thanked him in return for having them on, and left the studio.

On the way out, Pervis asked Lucky to stop by the radio station tomorrow if he got a chance, and Lucky agreed.

Pervis drove south and thought about the interview. He enjoyed it and felt it had gone well. It's a good thing Lucky was free tomorrow. He was anxious to get Lucky's take on the 'Glory Days'. Lucky was at Chess' new station in Milwaukee, WNOV for a while and was promoted from there to General Manager at WVON in 1970. This was after the death of Leonard Chess. He was only 52 when he passed. Right before he died, he installed a florescent WVON sign that could be seen throughout Chicagoland, especially on Lake Shore Dr. It was erected on top of their new office at 320 So. Michigan. Cecil Hale was also at WNOV, and was brought to WVON along with Jay Johnson, the last two full timers hired at WVON for a long time. 'Butterball' was shuffled back and forth between WVON and WNOV.

It was good to see the guys tonight again. And those memories! The sleepless sit in. That was something. In August 1964, there was a radio station promotion designed to raise funds for the SCLC (Southern Christian Leadership Conference), Dr. King's movement and Operation Breadbasket. Some of the management of SCLC, Operation Breadbasket, and WVON got together and came up with the idea that if

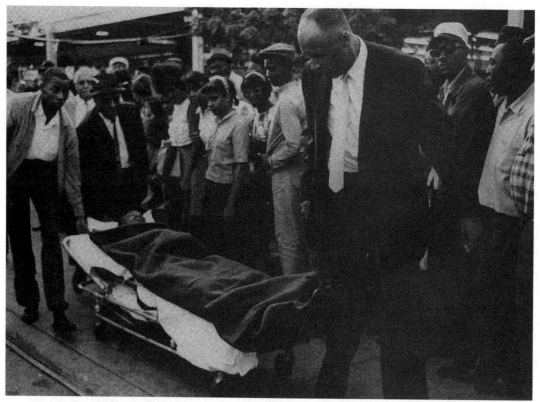

WVON Sleepless Sit-in

the disc jockeys would broadcast live for as long as they could, they could get a lot of people to donate to the cause, because money was so tight. Before it started, they thought they would raise about $4000 or $5000 and they would give that to Dr. King's organization. Leonard Chess thought it was a good idea. Since Operation Breadbasket was just an arm of SCLC, the largest portion of the revenue would go to SCLC. Operation Breadbasket was sponsored by King's movement, during the time when SCLC had a march going on in Jackson, Mississippi moving through Alabama. Jesse Jackson was here running Operation Breadbasket, what it was known by before PUSH.

The first day of the sleepless sit in, they took in about $5000 or $6000. The 'Good Guys' and WVON were so popular. They were the most popular thing going on in Chicago at the time and each disc jockey had his own following. If it was said, Herb Kent was going to be broadcasting from 35th and King Dr., Lake Meadows shopping center, at the big trailer, you can just come up and put your money in the basket that's out, and the money would go directly to SCLC, Dr. King's movement in order to deal with bond and things the King people had to put up to get out of jail, to pay attorney fees, and things of that nature, people would respond. All the DJs were at the trailer WVON had set up on 35th and King Dr., down at the northeast corner of the mall. Programming for the whole station was being operated directly from that particular spot. When Pervis came on at midnight, he stayed on until five o'clock in the morning. All the DJs were there and stayed there. The trailer was out for 87 & 1/2 hours, at least. It might have been longer than that, but that was how long he stayed awake. Pervis was the last person to go to sleep. There were always people out there, 24 hours a day. If anybody went to sleep, he got sent home. Rodney only stayed awake 24 hours. Pervis laid in the cut because most of those out there either drank or smoked or something. So he felt this wouldn't be too hard for him. Besides, he stayed up every night anyway, six or seven nights a week. Don Cornelious only stayed up ten or eleven hours. He didn't make it at all. Herb Kent did worse. Ed Cook, Rodney Jones, Bill "Doc" Lee, Cecil Hale, Butterball, Jay Johnson, and everybody else that was on the air was there. They had a doctor over there. After about eighty hours, he checked and looked at Pervis and asked him if he was all right. He said he was all right. Everyone else had given up the ship, something like 15 or 20 hours ago. Pervis was still up talking. He was doing something he really wanted to do, which was help the cause of freedom for Black folks. When it was over, they had raised more than $27,000. Instead of giving it all to Dr. King, they split it up between Dr. King, The Urban League, and the NAACP. There was no extra money for the DJs, they were just doing it for the cause of freedom, and Dr. King needed it to take care of his expenses, moving from place to place and the operation he was doing. The prize was the winner of this contest would have the chance to go to Jackson, Mississippi to march with Dr. Martin Luther King, Jr. Pervis didn't know it at the time. He didn't go. He was just too tired.

The next day, Lucky arrived and walked around to his former office, now occupied by Pervis.

"Spann, I am so glad you asked me to come by," Lucky said as he entered the office.

Pervis offered him a chair and headed to his favorite spot on the sofa.

"How's your wife Barbara doing?" asked Pervis,

"Barbara's doing very well, thank you," he replied.

"Lucky, you really look good."

"Pervis, I feel good."

"Looking back, what are some of your high points of being the manager here on radio station WVON?"

"Well, there are many Perv, and I'll try to remember some, but you lived them with me."

` "You kept me out of this room, because you locked the door."

"I didn't keep you out of this room. I had an open door policy, that door was never closed."

"You didn't have to close it in the morning. I worked nights. I was going to be at home sleep anyway," laughed Pervis. "But I was here for all your meetings."

"Yes you were," agreed Lucky. "I thought about the one we had here. The 'Good Guys' were right here, I was over

112

Lucky Cordell

there," Lucky gestured to a spot by the window. "That was the time when somebody had written a memo to downtown, saying all types of things about the jocks' behavior here at the station, that they were drinking and using drugs, when the bosses weren't around. They showed me the letter, and handed me this person on a silver platter. I could've fired the trick like this," he said with a snap of his fingers, "But I said to them at the corporate office downtown, 'look, this is a good jock, doing a good job at the station. This letter is all wrong, some bull'. So, I let him work until they sold the station. But the inside you don't know is once that same back stabbing jock came to me and asked if Barbara, my wife, would mind giving some pointers on where he and his wife should go when they visit Mexico. They'd never been out of the country, and Barbara and I had been there many times. So, I said sure, she'd be glad to. When I got home, I asked Barb, if she'd mind going back to Mexico with them as a guide to show appreciation to one of my top jocks. She said she loved Mexico, but had just gotten back. Then she said she'd go if I wanted her to. I told her he's one of my top jocks, no problem, he makes time, and I'd like to show him my appreciation. She asked who was going to pay for it. I said, I'm going to pay for it. She said I was something, and she sees why they, the jocks, love me. So, she went back with them."

"Did she know about the letter writing incident at the time?" asked Pervis.

"That was before the letter writing incident. The letter writing came afterwards," Lucky responded.

"Oh it came after?" Pervis asked with a raise of an eyebrow.

"Yea. So she goes to Mexico with them. They didn't have to do anything but get up. She had mapped out where they'd have lunch, sight see, high points, you know. And all while they were there he was telling her what a great guy I am. "Lucky's a great guy and blah, blah, blah...," and it wasn't two months later that I found out about the letter." Lucky paused then added, "now is that a snake doctor or what?"

"Hey, man, that's a snake doctor. I heard a little about it, but I never had the time to deal in other folks business," Pervis said. "So, since I didn't deal in other folks business, I had a little more time to take care of my own."

"I'll remind you of something. You should remember. Every once in a while I'd get a call from downtown," Lucky said. "They would go something like this: 'Lucky, good morning, this is George'.

'Oh, good morning George'.

'Listen, why was the switchboard operator late this morning'?

'She was late because she missed her bus and she doesn't drive. But the switch board was opened on time'.

'Well you know Lucky, you've got to stay on top of things like that. You can't let that go'.

"I just sat there and puzzled through it. How could he possibly know this? Does he have this place bugged? And on another occasion, he called me and he said, why did so-n-so leave before he finished his production time? I then knew, after a third incident, somebody down here is calling downtown. I found out that they had promised him, if ever I was no longer the manager, he'd get the job," said Lucky.

"Oh they did?" Pervis asked in surprise.

"They set him up," Lucky continued. "When you're weak, and someone tells you if 'this' happens you're going to get 'that', then you're going to try to make 'this' happen. I'll tell you when I busted him. Christmas, when we all got our last check, his check wasn't sent to me to distribute. So I called downtown and I said, 'Joe' that was the bookkeeper's name, 'I didn't get all the checks. There's one missing'. I told him who it was and he said, 'Ah, no, they said they're going to give it to him personally'. I said, 'look, the man wants his money, and he's out of town, so messenger it over to me'. And he did. You know why they didn't want to give it to me? They were paying him under the table. His salary, plus $1000. For $1000, he was selling us out."

Pervis gave a dry laugh.

"He fell out of the family," Lucky went on to say. "He went against the family. And to show you that things don't work like that, he never got the job. They used him up and tried to make him quit, and finally succeeded. They took him from the morning and put him on in the mid-day. That didn't make him quit. So they took him off the air as a disc jockey and put him in the news room. That didn't make him quit. So they hired this young 19 year old girl to be his boss. That got him."

"What girl was this?" inquired Pervis.

"Not here, of course. That's when they were downtown. I don't even know her name. After I was gone . . . , incidentally most people don't know, I was never fired. I've never been fired in my life. I resigned. I resigned because the new owners owned a boat company, sheet and tin mills, The Harlem Globetrotters, The Atlanta Braves, and seven radio stations. They were just a huge conglomerate and I was not to be affiliated with any of the radio stations. I was going to be assistant to the president of the corporation, and I was supposed to deal with the boat company and The Harlem Globetrotters. I'm a radio person. So I met with George Gillette, and I asked, 'can we talk openly'?, and he said,

'Sure.'

'I'm not happy', I said.

'What's wrong? You don't like your office, or secretary'? George asked.

"You know they moved me down to One IBM Plaza," explained Lucky

115

"I was unaware of that," Pervis admitted.

"They moved me down there with a big desk and two secretaries. And no power," Lucky finished.

"No power?" Pervis questioned.

"No power." Lucky repeated. "See, what had happened . . . I guess I'm getting a little ahead of myself," he said and went on to explain, "What happened was that they called me downtown. All this was before, "they," being George Gillette and Bob Bell, two of the conglomerate owners who bought the station from Leonard Chess, they called me downtown, and I'm going down there with a very positive attitude because I'm thinking they're calling me down there for a pat on the back at least, or maybe a little bonus. Our numbers were never better, the community loved us, and the employees were happy. So what would he call me downtown for? Its got to be something positive. I get downtown in the office, and I notice there's a somber attitude. George said, 'Lucky, we want to fire two disc jockeys'. I laughed. I said, 'You've got to be kidding'. He said no, they're very serious. I asked why would they want to fire two disc jockeys and which two? He said it didn't matter. I asked if he could tell me why and he said to cut the budget. I said, 'George I can't do that', and he asked, 'you refuse to do it?' I said, 'no I don't refuse, I can't. See when you leave here, One IBM Plaza, you go north. When I leave 33rd and Kedzie, I go further south. I am answerable to the community that we serve. I'll fire a man for a lot of things, insubordination, inability to make time, drugs. . . but I cannot go back to that radio station and just tap two guys on the shoulder and say we don't need you anymore. These men have made this station, made it worthwhile for you to buy it. They're buying homes, they have families'. Gillette said, 'in other words you won't do it'. I said they could fire me, they have the power. They could go out there and fire anybody they like. I can't do it. I knew he couldn't go around me. He had to go through me. They ended up deciding to table it for now. When I left their office and came and sat in my car, I thought, they're not through with this.

"I'd say two or three months later, I'm promoted without being consulted. Before I knew anything, photographers from *Jet* magazine arrived at my office taking pictures. That was to get me out of the position, so they could put someone in who would do their bidding. What do you call it, promote you up just to promote you out? Do you remember, Pervis, when you guys came to my home and sat in my living room and offered to walk when they promoted me, and I thanked you? I'll never forget it. You guys knew why they made this move. And I said fellows you're talking about walking, but a walk wouldn't have any meaning because in order for a walk to be successful, you've got to have the community behind you. What are you going to tell the community, you're walking because they promoted Lucky, because they moved him downtown and is now assistant to the president? The community would say, 'you're crazy. That's what we want for our people, to be promoted', What I want you to do for me is to go back and do the best job you can. Do your best. But be careful. Watch out for each other because they will come for you, one at a time.

"My job at this station was the happiest days of my life, in work. I was blessed to be able to work in radio my whole adult life. I never had another job after I got into radio. I used to sit in the parking lot out there when I had my check and peek to see if anybody was looking while I smiled and said. 'they pay me for this'?", said Lucky.

A laughing Pervis remarked, "you know this thing that you're telling me about, I didn't know. I never dug into what was going on."

"Well, you know, that's not your make-up. And the other thing was you were never around. By working the hours you worked, the only other time you'd come in was when we needed you for production work. So you wouldn't hear the whispering. But once they moved me downtown, I told George I wasn't happy. 'I know that you want to take control of the radio station,' I said to him. 'so why don't we agree to disagree.' He asked me what did I mean, and I said, 'I resign, and you pay me a year's salary'. He said, 'well I'm not saying I'd do that, but if I were agreeable, would you give me your word you wouldn't jam us in the media'? I said yea, so we shook hands on it and they paid me for a year in salary. The reason they asked me not to talk to the media is because I had everybody calling - The NAACP, the Urban League, PUSH, everybody was calling to find out about my so called promotion because it happened so fast. There was no publicity given, nothing, just boom, a picture in the

117

Jet that said Lucky Cordell promoted. They never came to me and asked, 'how would you like to move up'? I wasn't consulted, they just did it. And the same time they announced my move, they announced Bernadene's.

"I admire intelligence even if it's against me. When they kicked me upstairs, what did they do? They didn't replace me with a white, they replaced me with a Black woman. The community said, 'oh a Black woman'."

"Oh yes, this is double good," quipped Pervis.

"Yes," Lucky went on, "'Lucky's got a promotion and we've got a Black woman'. So they were shrewd. I marveled at them. Bern, in the capacity we had her in was doing an excellent job being an ambassador for the station, but for general manager, she was not qualified. When they promoted her downtown, the girl who was her secretary became her boss. Not to take anything away from Bern, they just used her. I can imagine conversations like, 'look, we're thinking about putting a lady in this position. Can you make tough decisions? You'll have to make some tough decisions'. Later they'd say, 'so you can make tough decisions, eh? We want you to eliminate two guys'. And it started to happen."

Bernadine Washington

Spann

"Well, I had my own thing. It was, Pervis mind your own business. Put on your shows. Do what you're doing with the FCC. I just stayed away from it."

"You were always an entrepreneur, an aggressive young man. I've always admired that. You kept something going all the time. If one thing didn't work, you'd go to another," Lucky said.

"We had that club over there on 55th and State, The Burning Spear, and it turned out to be a monster."

"Wait a minute. Are you talking about the one on Stony Island?"

"No. That was the other one after the one on State Street burned down."

"Yes, those were the days," said Lucky. "We were fortunate to have a boss like Leonard Chess. He had faith in all of us. One time he called me in his office and we were talking. He suddenly asked me how much I owed on my car. I don't remember the figure. Let's say it was $1500, because that was a long time ago. He pressed the intercom and said to his secretary, 'write a check out to Lucky Cordel for $1500'. I nearly fell out the chair. All I saw was Mafioso, he's going to own me. I said, Leonard, wait a minute. I can't . . . I don't know when I can pay that money back. I'll never forget his words. He said, 'Lucky, I believe in you. You'll make it. You have more talent in your little finger than most of the guys have in this whole city, and I'm betting you make it. You make it, you pay me back. If you don't make it, you don't owe me'."

"That's the way he was," Pervis agreed. "I could go to Leonard Chess almost any time. When I put on all those shows at the Regal, I could go, and Leonard would ask, "what do you need?" But he'd call me a name afterwards. I'd say I need $10,000. He'd tell that bookkeeper Adele to give me $10,000. After the show, I'd pay him back."

"Listen man, I've got to get out of here. As always, I enjoyed visiting with you. Everytime I come its like coming home."

"This is your home. This was your office for a long time. I remember when we used to have all of our meetings back here," Pervis said.

"All of them, right here," agreed Lucky.

"All the disc jockeys used to come back here."

Pervis walked Lucky the door and went back to his office.

V erlene entered her house and changed her cloths, slipping into something more comfortable. It was a long day and all she wanted to do was relax. Walking over to the VCR, she pushed the rewind button. She just barely had time to set the timer after Spann called to tell her when the interview was airing. She had a previous engagement that couldn't be missed, but was thankful for technology. As she poured a glass of wine, she reached over and pressed the play button.

After viewing the taped interview of Chicago Tonight celebrating the 40 year anniversary of WVON, Verlene felt herself slipping back in the day, back in time. Spann was right. If anyone should get credit for the Jackson 5, it should be him. And she could take credit for him discovering them. Verlene closed her eyes and remembered.

She and her husband, Clyde, had gone to Gary, Indiana to an affair. After the affair, they stopped to listen to another little group, which happened to be the Jackson 5. Clyde had enjoyed the show so well, he came back with them and asked Spann to put the young group on his talent show. At first, Spann didn't want them on his show. He said he didn't have time, but Clyde said, "man, I brought these guys all the way from Gary. Don't embarrass me. Would you just please put them on the show?" So Spann put them on the show, partly because of her and not to embarrass Clyde for bringing them all the way to Chicago. They got on the talent show and they won. They were fantastic, dynamic. They set the stage on fire. Michael couldn't have been older than five or six, and probably can't remember this now, but the daddy could remember it. They kept coming back and they kept winning the talent show. Then Spann started managing the Jackson 5, and picking up all their expenses. It got a little bit too expensive, Verlene understood. Maybe not at first, but there were 5 Jacksons, their daddy, a chaperone, and four or five band members. It got expensive when they were trying to eat, and to feed about 12 folks for lunch was really expensive during that time. Spann had to pay for them to get over here, buying gas and what not. The daddy worked in the steal mill, and they had one particular driver that would bring them over. Ms. Jackson would be there, and the little girls. This went on for quite some time. Verelene didn't see why Joe Jackson couldn't let the world know that those boys got their start and their exposure in Chicago by a Pervis Spann, and the Burning Spear. They stayed around for a while, and Spann was supposed to be the manager, with Joe Jackson the road manager, because he didn't know anything about the entertainment world. He just had some very talented sons, and they wanted to get going. After they performed for Spann on that stage, they set up that little deal where he and Joe signed a contract stating what they were supposed to do and what he was supposed to do. Verlene recalled asking Spann if he still had that contract, but he told her it would be no good because Joe had signed it, since the Jackson 5 were too young to sign, and that Joe couldn't sing a note. Some of the other places Spann had the Jackson 5 were the original Regal Theater, where the Jackson 5 did its last show before it closed in 1969, The Met on 46th and King Dr., The Capital Theater, and some smaller places like The Guys and Dolls, and lounges down in Joliet, Peoria and Cairo, Illinois.

Verlene sighed and thought if they knew then what they knew now. They should've had a journal of all the activities of everything and the dates. Oh well. That 20-20 hind sight was a trip. If she had a nickel for every act Spann and WVON's 'Good Guys' broke . . . Once the Jackson 5 signed on with Motown, WVON was first to get the records, and the

Janet and Joe Jackson

airplay took their career to the next phase. That radio station, WVON was one of a kind. It made so many artists popular. They promoted them and made numerous hit records, and people would come from far and near just to get their record played, knowing that once it was played on WVON, it was going to become a household name.

She laughed when she thought about Bob Sirott asking Spann on the Chicago Tonight interviews, if there was any artist he didn't get started, and Spann answered, without missing a beat, "It wouldn't be Al Green." They were doing so great at WVON, then the Burning Spear, Spann's club, that the mob came in to take over.

Verlene recalled one night they had a packed house at the Burning Spear, and the gangsters came in. She remembered this particular time, because then, they didn't have a lot of white people coming into the club. There were about three or four of them, and they were all well dressed,

124

Jackson 5 with Janet Jackson

Spann with Tyrone Davis and Al Green

wearing nice suits. The one thing that stands out in her mind is that they were looking out of place. The main one was a guy named Manny Scar and he was talking to Spann. She over heard him demanding a piece of the action. The Burning Spear was doing very well, and the reason why the mob knew how successful they were was because of the liquor houses. She would buy plenty of liquor for the club. They had to have liquor for their clientele. They had a lot of liquor. There was a front bar, a back bar, a lounge bar, and a reserve. Spann had always suspected the bartenders were stealing liquor, but Verlene knew they weren't stealing too much. She was a firing sister. Yes, they had many bartenders. Spann caught a few stealing. She caught a few stealing, but they didn't steal enough to make him poor. Spann had a saying about bartenders. He always said, show him a bartender and he'll show you a thief.

She never did hear Spann's response to Manny Scar, and she'd been meaning to ask him about it. On impulse, she picked up the telephone and dialed the station.

"Hello?"

"Hey Spann, how ya doin'?"

"Who's this?"

"It's me, Verlene."

"Oh hi Verlene."

"Are you busy?" she asked.

"No. I just got through talking to Lucky," answered Pervis.

"How is Mr. Cordell? I haven't seen him in ages," Verlene inquired. She always thought of him as a very sweet guy, one who she could certainly count on whenever she needed him.

"He's fine. We were going over some of the things that happened back in the day," he responded.

"Speaking of going over things that happened back in the day, do you remember when that gangster, Manny Scar came to the Burning Spear and tried to shake you down? I remember overhearing him asking you for a piece of the action. What did you say to him? I'd been meaning to ask you about that all these years, but kept forgetting," Verlene said.

"Manny Scar. Now what made you think of that? Let's see. Oh yes, I remember. I told him I'd get back to him. As a matter of fact, before that happened, one day I was sitting at the bar, you know the one that used to be the eating area when it was Club Delisa, the one we changed to the lounge?"

"Um hum," Verlene acknowledged, and Pervis continued.

"In walked two people, and I honestly didn't know who they were. I just knew there were two people, one big guy, kind of burley, and another one, pretty well dressed. It was springtime, either late spring or early summer. I was just sitting there talking to the staff, going over some of the things we were trying to accomplish. One of the guys walked up to me and said, 'you're Pervis Spann', and I said yes, and he said 'this is my district. I'm the commander. My name is Robert Hearnes'. I said, hello Mr. Hearnes. Then I discovered, a little later on, that he used to be 'Two Gun Pete's' partner. They used to ride in the squad car together. I know you remember 'Two Gun Pete'. He was allegedly, the meanest, the baddest, police man on the Chicago police force, barring none. That's the reputation he had, but I didn't know too much about Hearnes. I didn't know too much about 'Two Gun Pete', either. I didn't know too much about any of them. So, Hearnes said, 'looks like you're doing pretty good over here, Pervis.' I said, that yes I thought we were doing pretty well, could be better, could be worse, and that I was so thankful it was like what it was. Then he asked, 'did anybody come around and talk with you about going in business with you?" I said nobody had, and I had a partner named Rodney Jones. Commander Hearnes continued, 'no. I'm talking about did some white folks come through here'? I said no, and he said, 'well they're coming'. I told him I didn't know anything about it, and he said 'I'm telling you, they're coming'. I'd gathered that he had heard something I hadn't heard. He said, 'they will be through here'. I didn't worry too much about it because during the daytime hours, I was either at home sleep or out on the road giving a show, driving from town to town. I didn't know. So eventually the commander said, ' when they do come, tell them it's my place'. Then Hearnes thought for a while and said, 'I'll tell you what, I'm going to put two of my lieutenants over here as your security'. And that's what he did. He put 'Lock 'em up Jones' and another guy named Gus Lett. Gus Lett and 'Lock 'em up Jones' were dispatched to me at the Burning Spear. Commander Hearnes had said, 'when they

128

come to talk to you, let them talk to them', and he put them over there at the Burning Spear. When they came by to talk to me, they talked to Lett and Jones, except for that one time when I told Manny I'd get back with him," Pervis said.

"So that's how Lett and Jones came to be there. I always thought you set that up," Verlene said.

"No. They were there with Commander Hearnes compliments," said Pervis.

"I just got through watching the interview on Chicago Tonight. I taped it because I wasn't going to be home when it aired. It was an excellent show. It brought back a lot of memories. That's how I came to remember that Manny Scar person," Verlene recalled.

"Yes. He was affiliated with the Delisa's, the gangster family who used to own the Burning Spear, who were affiliated with Al Capone," he added.

"I got nervous when I heard that Manny Scar person talking to you because of the time you told me about the Leonard Chess incident when he was all beat up," Verlene mentioned.

"Oh yes," Pervis said. "That was the time Leonard Chess had all kinds of scars and bruises on him. I wanted to know what had happened. This was before WVON really got going. It looked liked somebody had put a real beating on him, like they tried to kill him. Finally, I got around to asking some of our friends what happened to him. They said, well some of the gangster friends got a hold of him and left him in that condition. They were trying to kill him. Now I don't know who it was. Some people told me that it was the Manny Scar outfit, and some folks said it was just some hooligans. Somebody did it either for records or money. I don't know. Leonard Chess had a run in with somebody. Were they trying to beat him up because he had got a radio station and turned it all Black? What was it that they were trying to beat Leonard Chess to death about? He had the whole blues scene in Chicago completely rapped up. Leonard never spoke a word of it to me; therefore, I played it off. He wasn't dead, and things seem to be going well with the station."

"I remember that time clearly, because it really shook me up. You had come in the Burning Spear one afternoon and-"

"Sorry to interrupt," Pervis cut in, "but it's getting to be that time."

Verlene looked at the bird clock on the wall. Every hour a different type of bird would cheep out the time. "Oh my, is it that late?" Verlene asked as the first chirp began to cheep out the midnight hour. "Okay, Spann, I'll talk to you soon."

Verlene remembered to place the cordless phone on the base, and headed for the steps. Quietly, she made her way to her room and bed. Her husband was already asleep.

Lucky him, she thought an hour later as she lay staring into the darkness. Suddenly she sat bolt upright in bed. What was that noise? She kept quiet but heard nothing. It must have come from outside she figured, as she returned to a reclining position. All that talk about Manny Scar and Al Capone must have got her keyed up. And the memories . . .

As she traveled in time, Verlene let her thoughts become her bedtime story; but, this was no story. It was real.

Spann had come into the Burning Spear one afternoon, very excited. Along with the usual promotions and games WVON was famous for, they had the opportunity to sponsor one of the greatest entertainers in the Black arena anywhere at that time, Mr. Sam Cooke. Sam Cooke was hot, WVON was hot, and had come up with the promotion whereby they were going to give a show with Sam Cooke, and a few others. Miller High Life wanted to sponsor the program. They would present the show, pay for it, and WVON would be the promoter, and advertise it. It was to be at White Sox park. Also on the show would be Albert King, Stevie Wonder, Marvin Gaye and others, right there on 35th and Shield, in Chicago, in the park. They were putting it together under the direction of Miller High Life beer. If people won tickets on the station, they, of course, wouldn't have to pay to get in. They also had a little thing going where Miller would give coupons if a person bought some of their beer.

Verlene remembered how excited Pervis and Rodney were the days and weeks leading up to the event. Sixty thousand people showed up, and many of them ended up standing, because the park wouldn't hold sixty thousand seated. It was actually a promotion for WVON and Miller beer. So many folks were in attendance there, and the coupons they got from Miller beer were admittance to the show. It was a marvelous performance. Stevie Wonder was a young man, about 15 or 16 years old.

Sam Cooke

They also had a big, tall guy by the name of Albert King. He played a lot of blues. It was one of the biggest shows that had ever been in Chicago. The crowd there really enjoyed that concert. Everybody had fun. This was another feather in Spann's cap because promoting the show under the direction of WVON and Miller High Life beer gave him two vital, strong sponsors, and it really worked. It's all people talked about prior to and then after. Sam Cooke put on a masterful performance. He was really sizzling that night. Its been said when people put on their best show, it's usually their last. He put on one before the hometown folks at Sox Park and turned it out. That was his last big concert appearance in his lifetime. It was like they were playing the super bowl and somebody caught the last winning touchdown in the game, when Sam Cooke hit that stage.

After the show was over, everyone went their own way. About a couple of months later, they heard that Sam Cooke had met with a tragedy in Los Angeles, CA. He was assassinated. Nobody knew the exact circumstances. They knew Sam Cooke was an enterprising young man. Born in Clarksdale Mississippi, but raised in Chicago, he proved yet again a lot of the Mississippians are enterprising young people. Sam Cooke was with the RCA Victor label. He had threatened not to re-sign with them. His contract had just run out. Sam had formed his own label. He had a guy working with him by the name of Bobby Womack. Bobby signed with Sam and was playing for him. Then he had the Simm twins, a couple of singers, and four or five other artist including Johnnie Taylor. Sam Cooke was going to be publishing and writing his own material. It was something, at that time of life, almost unbelievable, and real innovative for a Black man to be forming his own record company. He was a good looking young fellow, slim, and had the best voice that you could ever find in a human being anywhere. Sam was a threat to everybody out there that was singing and producing. He had already taken over all the top spots in America as far as Black music was concerned.

No one really knows exactly what happened. Speculation was that the person they accused of killing Sam Cooke was a female. They accused her of killing him, but Spann, Verlene knows, always had his doubts, then and now. How come after she killed Sam Cooke, Spann used to ask, she died so suddenly herself? Just what was really going on in that arena? After Sam Cooke was shot, his body was shipped back to Chicago to A.R. Leak's Funeral Home. Spann attended that funeral. It was a cold day. Verlene remembered that there were so many people, that they almost couldn't find a place big enough to have a funeral for him, but they managed. Services for Sam Cooke were held at Tabernacle Church on 42nd and Indian, officiated by Rev. Rawls. After it was over, the body was shipped back to Los Angeles. What Spann found out later via autopsy, and something that did not get out to the public, was that Sam Cooke had a broke arm at the time of death. Spann always contended, just tussling around with a prostitute would not give one a broke arm. Knowing how this business worked, Spann came to the conclusion that Sam Cooke, because of the things he was doing, setting up his own publishing company, taking care of all his business as far as singing and writing was concerned and had other folks signing with his record label, met with the same fate as Leonard Chess, but his fatal. Spann had gone on record saying the gangsters murdered Sam.

This had sent chills up Verlene's spine at the time. She usually opened the Burning Spear and closed up, sometimes alone. Walking up to the door about a week after Sam's death, Verlene put her key in the lock to enter the club. Just as she got the door opened and entered, she felt cold, rough hands close around her throat and push her into the Burning Spear. As the hands squeezed tightly, cutting off her wind, she managed to turn and see Manny Scar's face just before loosing consciousness.

Verlene woke up gasping for breath, drenched in sweat. She just had a terrible dream. How could long buried memories cause her to have nightmare so vivid? She can't even remember falling asleep. Her last thoughts were of the horrible time Sam Cooke was murdered, and how Spann likened it to the Leonard Chess beating.

She got out of bed and went to get a cool glass of water. After drinking the liquid and taking several deep breaths, Verlene felt herself getting back to normal. She sat down in her plush recliner and picked up where she left off with her last conscious thought. She had the feeling if

Bobby Womack

she did not bring closure to these memories in her mind, she would never be able to sleep comfortably.

Sam Cooke did not have to go out and solicit or seduce a prostitute, since he was one of the most popular Black entertainers in the whole country during that time. Spann had said if Sam was second, he didn't know who was first. He also used to say, Sam Cooke's life was not one of dealing with prostitutes. Women were always flocking all over him, anywhere in the country. With prostitutes then, you only needed about three to five dollars for services. It didn't make any since to Spann and it didn't make any since to her. The investigation into Sam Cooke's death was wiped out after the demise of the lady in Los Angeles who was allegedly responsible for it, which brings up suspicions as to what really did happen to Sam Cooke.

She recalled Spann sadly saying that Sam Cooke had only gotten to the point of singing a few of his favorite songs. He never did get all of his recordings where he should have gotten them before he left here and went to be with the lord. A man with his voice, looks and charisma never did reach the plateau he thought Sam could have, and Spann knew he was destined to be the best entertainer on the Black circuit. That was already a foregone conclusion. People from far and wide always marveled at the charisma, voice and talent he possessed throughout the tenure of his career. Spann's opinion was that Sam Cooke was one of the greatest to ever come through this life, and Verlene agreed.

She shifted positions in her chaise lounge. Oh yes, she remembered that time well. Not too long after the Sam Cooke mystery, WVON got immersed in one of its own. This one effected her.

Verlene will never forget that day. She was driving to work, the Burning Spear. As usual, she had WVON on the radio. There was announcement made. The worst had happened. E. Rodney Jones, Program Director and co-owner of the Burning Spear was missing. Someone had kidnapped him. As she drove, she felt as if all the blood were being drained from her body. She hoped Spann would be there. She stepped on the gas and doubled up her efforts to get to the club.

As Verlene made her way across the city, how she first met Rodney came to mind. One time Spann had a show at The Packing House. She

135

didn't recall who was on the show, but Rodney came to the bar and he wanted a drink, and he didn't pay. After telling him that he would have to pay for his liquor, Rodney kindly informed her he was Spann's partner. Verlene then told him she didn't know anything about it, and he had to pay. Finally, Spann came over and told her that Rodney was his partner in this show and that he doesn't have to pay. That was when she first saw and met Rodney, at The Packing House.

Rodney had not been in Chicago long. He worked at a radio station over on the west side, WYNR. She remembered him telling her and Spann they got rid of him over at WYNR because his voice sounded too Black. They got rid of all the Black sounding folks over there, and replaced them with white sounding Negroes so they could reach a bigger audience. After they fired him over there, he came to WVON. Rodney wasn't in the circle at the time Spann first started his shows.
She turned into the parking lot of the club and raced inside. Thank goodness Spann was there.

"Spann, I heard on the way over here Rodney was kidnapped. People were calling in crying. I knew that Manny Scar character wasn't to be trusted. Did you notify Commander Hearnes?" Verlene asked as she ran in breathless.

"Calm down, calm down. What are you all worked up about?" Pervis questioned.

"It's Rodney. They've got him," she exclaimed. "Manny Scar has kidnapped Rodney."

"You say Rodney Jones is missing?"

"Not just missing, kidnapped. I heard Roy Wood on the news on my way over here," Verlene said, between breaths.

"What? You're kidding," Pervis said, looking shocked at Verlene. "We've got to do something. Call the police, no the National Guards, the CIA, somebody," Pervis said to an almost hysterical Verlene.

As she began to race to the phone, she noticed a twinkle in Spann's eye. She took another look and saw his lip quiver.

"Spann, what's going on?" she asked accusingly.

"Missing, kidnapped, however it was. It doesn't seem right to me that something could happen to Rodney." Pervis said with a grin. "They can't

136

find him? Don't worry about it. It's probably a contest going on at the radio station and they're looking for Rodney. It must be a publicity stunt that WVON is pulling. The promotion staff comes up with ideas. It is their obligation to invent things of that nature.   I heard talk about something like this; but, I wasn't sure they were actually going to go through with it. So, I would not be too concerned about Rodney Jones missing. He'll turn up sooner or later if it's Rodney, 'cause he's kind of playful anyway. Don't worry about it. If it was something very serious, Commander Hearnes and some of the other folks would be on top of it. If you hadn't heard anything from the police department, don't worry about it. Rodney is more or less a lady's man, so if I were you, I wouldn't be too concerned," Pervis explained.

Verlene stood there, gaping at Pervis.

"How dare you string me along," she said through clinched teeth. "Why didn't anybody tell me about this? I work with you and Rodney everyday, and nobody mentioned this stunt to me? You know how shook up I've been since Manny Scar has been on the scene, then the Sam Cooke tragedy. Why didn't you warn me?"

"I'm sorry, Verlene. Once I saw how upset you were, I couldn't take the joke any further. As you just alluded to, so much has been going on. I guess it just slipped my mind," Pervis apologized. "Anyway, Manny Scar won't be kidnapping anybody. I just learned he was found dead, bullet hole in the head."

Verlene came back to reality and noticed she actually felt as if she could sleep for hours. The calmness that enveloped her after Spann reassured her Rodney was okay seemed to extend to her earlier agitated state now. She left her Lay-Z-Boy and got back into bed. Before she had time to dwell any more on the past, a deep restful sleep engulfed her being.

Pervis entered his office and immediately was greeted by the ringing of the telephone. He picked up the receiver.

"Hello"?

"Hey Spann, it's me Verlene. I was just calling you to see if you heard about the death of Nina Simone. Since Rodney used to have her perform at the Burning Spear, I thought you might be interested.

"No, I hadn't heard anything yet. I just got in. What happened"? Pervis asked.

"The only details I have is that she died in her home in France, where she was currently residing," Verlene responded.

"Yes, Rodney was responsible for bringing Nina Simone to the Burning Spear more than one time. He and Nina Simone appeared to have had a relationship like me and Aretha Franklin. Whatever she wanted to do, he was for it. Whatever he wanted her to do, she was for it; therefore, we got a chance to meet her and do some great things with her. It was a stupendous relationship with one of the greatest singers that ever lived, Nina Simone," said Pervis.

"Well, I was just calling to let you know

Jones and Spann

I'll talk to you later," Verlene said and rang off.

Pervis sat behind his desk and pick up the phone again. This time he was making the call.

"Hey Rodney, it's me, Spann, how are you?"

"Not bad buddy, how about you?"

"Fine. I was just calling because your name came up. I was talking to Verlene and we were discussing the passing of Nina Simone. Of course your name would come up," Pervis said.

"Yes, I heard about that. She was a great lady," Rodney remembered. "A legend."

"I knew you two were close," admitted Pervis.

"We were. I hadn't spoken to her in years, though, every since she left the U.S. in 1973 because of the racism here. May she rest in peace," Rodney finished sadly.

Pervis agreed with the sentiment, and continued, "it's good you're felling better, Rodney."

"I feel stronger and I'm under the doctor's care. I'm careful not to do anything I'm not supposed to do," said Rodney.

"It's too bad you're not able to come in from Baton Rouge for the 40 years' festivities. Of course, your health is more important, but I miss you. Especially the other night when we were on Chicago Tonight with Bob Sirott, you might remember him. He used to be on WLS radio. Anyway he interviewed Lucky, Herb, Wesley, and me about the glory days. I really wish you could have been there. You could have shed some light on a few things," Pervis said.

"Oh yea? What did you all talk about?" Rodney asked.

"Basically how influential WVON was in the '60s and '70s, in terms of making artists famous, and the civil rights movement," Pervis responded.

"Oh yea, they tried to tear up the West Side April 4, 1968, after Martin Luther King Jr. was assassinated. You know we were on the air for about 18 hours straight, talking to the people about not tearing up their neighborhood and destroying where they live. Mayor Daley was not going to let them near downtown. They could forget that. He had the National Guard all around the loop, Wacker Dr., State Sreet and Michigan Avenue. We did 18 hours straight talk, no music, just begging Negroes not to tear

WVON Cadillac

up their place, but they still destroyed a lot of things on the West side, not nearly as much on the South side. I would say we curbed the violence by at least 40%, by getting on the air talking to those people," Rodney said.

"We talked about the sleepless sit-in on Chicago Tonight, too. How many hours did you stay woke, Rodney?" asked Pervis.

"Oh, hell, you know I went to sleep. I stayed up less than 24 hours, I know that," Rodney laughed.

"Rodney, how about that girl that found you?", Pervis asked, referring to the time the radio station did the promotion where Rodney was missing. He remembered Verlene's reaction when she found out about it, but hers was nothing compared to the callers. They would phone the station crying and screaming, especially the women. Some men were concerned also, but the women where truly besides themselves.

"She was right there working at that Walgreen, right there in Lake

Meadows. That's where I walked in and the girl grabbed me. Do you know who she is? The girl that's got the lounge, the 50 Yard Line. That's who found me," replied Rodney.

"Okay. Did she really find you or you found her?" Pervis asked.

"She found me when I walked in the door. She grabbed me and started screaming. But that's who that was. Her name was Willa Mae, the girl who owns the 50 Yard Line, her and her football player husband. They've got a club on 79th, I think or 75th Street, one of the two, and they also had a 50 Yard Line out there in the suburbs, too," Rodney said.

"Well she won the $500 reward the station was giving to anyone who could find you. Who was the girl that won the Cadillac?" Pervis asked.

"I can't think of her name, man. I remember her, but I can't think of her name."

"What year Cadillac was that?" Pervis wanted to know.

"All that was between '63 & '70," Rodney answered.

"Looks like it was a '64 or '65 Cadillac," Pervis suggested.

"Yea, '64 or '65 would be good timing. Most of the stuff that we're talking about is between the time we hit the air, which was '63 up until '70. That's when it started tapering off and we were not doing as much," Rodney said.

"Well, that's about all we talked about on TV. I hope you continue to get better." Pervis said.

After catching up on a few other things, Pervis bid his friend and partner good-bye, and hung up the phone.

Yes, WVON had some wildly popular games and contest at that time.

"Buzz," his intercom sounded.

"Yes?"

"It's me Daddy," Pervis heard Melody's melodious voice come through the speaker. He marveled for the millionth time at his daughter's voice that so appropriately matched her name. The earthy huskiness continued, "You won't believe who I have in my office. It's one of the original contest winners of a Cadillac from one of the promotions the 'Good Guys' had'.

"Ask him to come in my office before he leaves," Pervis requested.

The old school spirit continued to link past with present and allow

Pervis' thoughts to become things.

As the gentleman entered his office, Pervis thought he didn't look old enough to have been around back then.

"Sit over here," he motioned to the man. "What's your name?"

"Maza Gerald May," Pervis thought he heard him say.

"Who?" he asked.

"Mazzar Gerald Mangun."

"How old are you?" asked Pervis.

"I'm fifty-three," Mazzar answered.

"No you're not," said Pervis in disbelief.

"Oh yes I am," Mazzar admitted.

"Alright. How long did that Cadillac last?" Pervis asked him.

"I kept that Cadillac four years, then I sold it," said the contest winner.

"What Cadillac are you talking about?" inquired Pervis.

"It was the Cadillac I won off of radio station WVON in 1967. It was white with a black top convertible. It was one of the best driving cars I ever had," Mazzar said.

"Well, how come you didn't keep it but for four years?" Pervis wanted to know.

"I just got into some other stuff, and then I just sold it," he responded.

"What did you do to win the Cadillac?" asked Pervis.

"It was a contest and you had to guess the weight of the staff of WVON and two mystery gifts in the trunk. After about a month or so, no one could come close to winning it, and they would tell you if you were too high or too low. So I called in," he explained.

"You kept calling in, didn't you?" Pervis asked.

"I kept calling in. I had to be very persistent. I made about 50 calls," Mazzar said.

"But you finally made it," Pervis said.

"Yes I did," Mazzar admitted.

"Boy. That's strange because however you did it, it was a good job and I'm happy and proud that you won it. I was wondering who it was that won that car. As a matter of fact, we had your picture on the wall. We were trying to find out just who did win that car. What's your mama's name?"

145

"Dorothy," he said.

"Dorothy, what?" Pervis asked.

"Dorothy Bobbitt," Mazzar answered.

"What was it then?" Pervis went on to question.

"It was Dorothy Bobbitt then."

"Okay, all right. So you were how old when you won?" asked Pervis.

"I was 17 years old."

"You were too young to drive a Cadillac," Pervis said.

"At that time, you could get your driver's license at 15, and I had my drivers license for two years and no car to drive. I graduated high school that June, and I believe I won the car that July."

"Give me your phone number, please," requested Pervis.

Once he was gone, Pervis was reminded about that other car that was won by a friend of Rodney's.

Apparently, Rodney had told one of his girls where the key was. The object of the contest was to listen to clues on the radio and find the key to the Cadillac, which was hid behind a billboard on Roosevelt Road. Leonard was mad as hell he had to give that car up, thanks to Rodney's assistance.

Another lady won a Pontiac, from Al Abrahms, and students could win money for having a lucky notebook sticker.

Radio station contests came and went. The next particular one that

had listeners in a frenzy was the one that pitted disc jockeys against each other. Pet Milk sponsored a contest where each DJ would ask people to save the labels off the Pet Milk cans and send them in to the radio station. Sometimes it would be so many labels. The one that always won that Pet Milk contest was the guy that did the gospel program by the name of Bill "Doc" Lee because mamas would go out and do the shopping, and they'd get the Pet Milk. Sometimes people would go in the grocery stores, and instead of buying the can of milk, they would just rip the label off of it and keep going. Whichever disc jockey that had the most labels from the Pet Milk can would win a TV set. Pervis never did win. Whatever listener that would send in the most labels would also win a color TV.   Even though 'VON was already number one, there was always something going on at the radio station that would keep them number one.

Whenever a station wants to get some listeners in a hurry, give some

money away. They will come. WVON had a contest where people could come to the station and give up two dollars and get five dollars. So WVON had it so designed that when they came up in the parking lot, they had to go around in a circle. It would be so many folks in the line that they couldn't go back to the end of the line because if they came in one way, 31st street for example, they'd come in the parking lot and get sent south. They had to go across that bridge. It was a bridge there then, which had two lanes, one for the north and one for the south. During that time there was no expressway. They'd have to drive three hours, seemed like, to get back around to get back in that line again. It was fun and people were talking about it. All of this went on before the sale of WVON.

148

In the late '60s or early '70s, WVON was sold by
Leonard Chess to Globetrotter Communications,
another Jewish organization. At that time, they had a rule
at the FCC that you could only have one AM station in the
market place, and one FM station in the market place.
Pervis thought it was a very good idea because Black folks
would stand a better chance of acquiring a license, if it
remained that way. So, after WVON was sold to
Globetrotter, they turned around and bought another AM
station, and therefore owned two stations in one market
place, 1450 AM and 1390 AM; but, the rules of the FCC
said you could only own one AM station and one FM
station. It's not like that any more now. Thanks to the
Telecommunications Reform Act, one can own as many
stations in one marketplace as one could purchase.
The current law suggest they could raise the prices on the
stations, on the big ones, to the point where even if a
person wanted to buy a station, it would cost him dearly
because he'll have to compete in the same market place
with conglomerates owning several channels. It was so
designed that the deck was stacked against a small firm,
and continues to be, even today.

150

The FCC made the new WVON owners divest themselves of one of their licenses. Globetrotter Communications found a potential buyer; but, The FCC uncovered some skeletons in his closet, and gave Globetrotter only so much time to find a new one. During the time of the changing of ownership, it was business as usual at the station, until Globetrotter wanted to move the 1450 frequency to the 1390 frequency, which was prohibited by the rules and regulations of the federal government. In order to do that, they would have to own both frequencies at the same time. They had that one company, one license rule. When Globetrotter got to the point where they had to comply with the, then rules of the Federal Communications Commission, they couldn't. Before the deal was closed, they had to divest themselves of one of the frequencies, so they got rid of the 1450 frequency because that was only 1000 watts, but kept the WVON call letters they owned, along with the 5000 watt 1390 frequency. In divesting themselves of the 1450 frequency, it was sold to a Mexican group. Then, the FCC found that the Mexican group wasn't in compliance;. therefore, when it was time to close, they couldn't. This put the FCC in a bind. They couldn't give Globetrotter any more time to search for buyers. So, the FCC took back the 1450 frequency for re-issuing. When they did, a number of people filed applications for that license, some Black, some white, some Mexicans. It was a total of about eight applications, and Pervis and his group, Midway Broadcasting, was one of the applicants. Midway Broadcasting was comprised of Pervis Spann, Wesley South, and some other shareholders. Acquiring WVON was Pervis' idea, and no one else. He was the only one with the money.

Pervis continued to work at WVON, even though the frequency was now 1390. He was still the all night blues man, but things just weren't the same. As time went by, many of the former 'Good Guys' were being replaced by new disc jockeys. At some point, white folks dealing with Blacks have the tendency to want to remove the original Blacks for one reason or another. Maybe white folks think they've been with them too long, or that people want to hear a different voice, or whatever the reason. They own mostly all the frequencies anyway.

So, when WVON changed hands, they did like most new owners do, they brought in the hatchet person, and that hatchet person didn't really know anybody at the radio station. It didn't matter how good you used to be on the station or who listened to you. The new owners figured that people were going to listen anyway because the station was going to play music, and folks will listen to the music. They just didn't care. The personality didn't mean anything to the hatchet person. They used it on the likes of Rodney Jones. Lucky was already gone. That's always some of the first people they get rid of. Lucky was manager at that time. As a rule, the first to go, generally, is the management.

Things started to get more and more uncomfortable for Pervis at WVON under new ownership. Once they discovered they couldn't control him, they started to make his stay as uncomfortable as possible. They began to withhold his wages, under the guise of money due them for his advertisement of the shows he was bringing into the Burning Spear. Pervis didn't blink. He was making so much money promoting acts that he didn't even give them the pleasure of requesting his checks. Once they saw they couldn't get to him that way, they started trying to force him to take his pay, but even then, he wouldn't cash their checks.

Finally, Globetrotter Communications sold the station to Combined Communications. With the station, they inherited its management style. Two weeks after Combined took over, they fired Pervis. Two weeks after that, Pervis slapped them with a lawsuit. The headlines of the May 5-7 1978 Chicago Citizen Weekend Newspaper, in big bold print read:
Spann Sues WVON - Fired DJ asks $1 Million - Page 3

Following is the story as it appeared in its entirety.

Pervis "The Blues Man" Spann filed suit against radio station WVON for more than $1 million Monday. Spann, whose midnight disc jockey show began when WVON was founded, April 1, 1963, was fired two weeks ago without prior notice. Joseph D. Jones, Black president and general manager of WVON since Combined Communications of Phoenix, AZ took over April 12, reportedly charged Spann with "conflict of interest." The apparent "conflict" is that Spann, WVON talk show host Wesley South, Chicago Tribune columnist Vernon Jarrett and other prominent Chicago

Blacks have applied to the Federal Communications Commission to operate a radio station on the 1450 AM frequency formerly held by WVON.

"What's wrong with Blacks wanting to own a radio station?" asked Spann in a Weekend interview Tuesday. "I'm nothing but a whipping boy."

Claiming he has been misquoted in the press, while refusing to be specific about the claim, Jones responded to the suit. "I don't know if I should answer any questions. I have not read the brief, but I have heard about it."

The suit contends that WVON owes Spann $72,000 for the following: $15,000 severance pay guaranteed by his union contract, $4000 vacation pay, $32,000 wrongfully billed and forcibly collected from Spann for alleged advertising in connection with Spann's promotion at his Burning Spear night club, $8,000 in advertising commissions, $13,000 for lost profits caused by WVON wrongs. Also the suit asks for $100,000 damages for injury to Spann's "reputation, mental and physical well being caused by WVON's intentional and malicious attack upon him and his economic livelihood."

In addition, it asks the court to award Spann $500,000 in punitive damages and $500,000 as exemplary damages. "Firing me is one thing," says Spann, "but then to take my money and try to put me out of business as a promoter is another." According to Spann's complaint flied in Circuit Court on his behalf by Atty. Edward Vrodolyak, alderman (D-10th). Globe Broadcasting, the Chicago based conglomerate which preceded Combined Communications as owner of WVON, threatened Spann with "loss of his job if he objected or filed a grievance with his union" over withheld wages applied to alleged debts for advertising on WVON. The complaint further contends that "billings for advertising and productions for Black artist performing in the Chicago area, which were not the product, property, or responsibility of (Spann) had been billed to (Spann) by WVON.

Moreover, it claims that at the time of Spann's discharge, Jones demanded "immediate payment of $6,000 for advertising (allegedly) owed to the station, and threatened to put Spann out of business." It adds that WVON refuses to accept any advertising from Spann since his dismissal. Consequently, though Spann paid $796 in cash on April 17, 1978 for 23 advertising spots to be broadcast by WVON to publicize his Bobby Bland show of April 19 to 22, the ads were never aired. As a result, Spann lost $13,000 in that promotion.

In that same edition, there was another story about a relatively unknown disc jockey, that quit at WVON because they tried to change his morning drive time to that of the blues man old time slot at midnight. Tom Joyner was his name, who is now Black America's most reknown disc jockey. He, subsequently, went over to WJPC.

In the mean time, Pervis took a job at an FM station. He went over to a good FM station. They had not too long ago gained popularity. At first,

Tom Joyner (3rd from left) and Chic

154

most radios only came with an AM signal. Once people were able to get a radio with both AM & FM, they began buying new ones. All the automobiles had begun to install AM/FM radios in stereo. FM became very popular, and people started gravitating to the FM market. After a while, stations like WVON, and any other station on the AM band began to loose some of its glamour. Folks could hear that good sound coming out of FM, and stopped listening to AM.

The FM station Hoffman gave to Chess for a $1, WSDM, was sold to the new owners for five million dollars. Pervis and the others used to call it their sister station. It hadn't anybody on it but females, no males. Many of the founding women of radio got their start there, such as Linda Ellerbee, Yvonne Danials, and Wonda Wells. All women operated that station, and they had fairly good listeners. Whatever they did diluted some listeners from the old WVON. Everything they were doing on the FM band meant that they were going after listeners, and wherever they could get them, they took them.

After a period of about five years, the FCC finally granted the Black folks one half of the license, which turned out to be the WVON portion, and they granted the white folks the other half of the license. Before they granted WVON one half of the license, the other 52 radio stations in Chicago were owned by whites. John H. Johnson then bought a radio station called WGRT with a Black format, and changed the call letters to WJPC. Those were the only two radio stations, rather station and a half out of 54 stations in the city of Chicago, owned by Blacks. So when they granted one half of the 1450 frequency to the Blacks, which was Midway Broadcasting, they couldn't use the call letters WVON because WVON was now 1390. Midway Broadcasting changed the call letters temporarily to WXOL. WXOL, in itself, didn't stand for anything in particular, but they were the new call letters at the AM 1450 frequency. One can't get call letters that other folks have, it doesn't matter what part of the country they may be in. If they own those call letters, a person has to get some other call letters. WXOL, they found out, was open so those were the ones they used. That was one reason they used WXOL.

When the FCC granted Midway Broadcasting the frequency 1450, they couldn't just get back on the air because Combined Communication owned the tower. Even though Midway Broadcasting now had the license, they didn't have a tower and didn't have a place to broadcast from. Combined, however, was pretty good to them, despite the pending lawsuit. They agreed to let Midway come into the building WVON now occupies, if they could find a place for a studio. Their equipment house was directly behind it, always had been, and the tower was there, too. So they set up their studio in what is now Pervis' office. On his desk, they laid out all the broadcasting equipment, turntables and what not, until they got enough money to go out and buy some other things. Everything else belonged to Combined. Midway barely had anything, but because they had already been dealing with Combined, they were gracious enough to let them come in their spot and broadcast WXOL.

They went on the air, and started doing what they were doing a long time ago with WVON, but they just didn't have enough time to do it, because what happened was in order for them to get that license, they had to cut a deal with the McGowans (the other group that got granted half of the license) whereby Midway would have to share time on the frequency.   McGowans came in and did Polish and other foreign programming. Midway (WXOL) did 15 hours a day of Black programming, and McGowan Communications was doing nine hours the weekdays, all day Sunday and Saturday afternoon.

When they came back on the air as WXOL, they brought in the number one Black disc jockey for gospel, Bill "Doc" Lee. Wesley South and Pervis Spann were the chief operators there. Of course, Pervis took the all night show, and Wesley South talking, assumed from ten to twelve o'clock p.m., because on first run at WVON, he only had the one hour and he wanted two, which was fine with Pervis.   They also had Rodney Jones, the WVON program director who worked with them for a little while, until they got squared away.   Many of those 'Good Guys' that were put out of work by the big conglomerates that came through, got another chance. Ed Cook worked there with them, (who by the way, had married Bernadine C. Washington) and Lucky Cordel returned.   They also brought in a couple of new guys. One was a guy by the name of, or who called himself 'Marvelous' Marvin Henry. Another called himself the 'real' Bob Jones. The real Bob Jones got killed after they were on the air for a little

The WXOL Family

Bill "Doc" Lee, *host of the Gospel Hour*

Pervis Spann, the Blues Man, *Operations Mgr. & Gen'l Sales Mgr.*

E. Rodney Jones, the "Mad Lad"

Wesley South, *News and Editorial Director (General Manager)*

Roy Wood, *Commentator*

Lucky Cordell, *Blues Specialist*

Ed Cook, "The Nassau Daddy"

"Marvelous" **Mark Hendricks**

"The Real" **Bob Jones**

Kitty Neely

Bill "Butterball" Crane

Chicago's Only Blues Station

WXOL
1450 AM 3350 South Kedzie Avenue Chicago, Illinois 60623 312/247-6200

while, at a lounge on the west side. There was a lady, Kitty Neely, who used to work with Pervis over at WXFM, and was one of the dancers at his Club, one of the Bill Cody dancers. After they got on the air at WXOL, she came over, then ended up at WJPC. Kitty who was a very sweet lady, went on to soul heaven also. Another lady who came over was Ms. Verlene Blackburn. She became Pervis' personal assistant. They had a very small staff of people and Verlene, who had never been in radio before, did what she saw needed to be done. She began writing commercials, producing, and anything else that had to be taken care of. Bill 'Butterball' Crain was there working because he was just so good, a really marvelous individual. He came over and worked with them for a little while. The on air personalities were Bill 'Doc' Lee, Pervis Spann, E. Rodney Jones, Wesley South, Roy Wood, Lucky Cordell, Ed Cook, Mark Henry, The 'Real' Bob Jones, Kitty Neely, Ed Cook and Bill 'Butterball' Crain, which made a real good staff. They operated like that for quite a while, from that room. WXOL never really took off like the original WVON, but they hung in there. It was like a brand new station, even though they had most of the 'Good Guys' back, and like a new station, the first year was rough. As the years went by revenue picked up, and they always got paid on time.

The law suit was finally settled, and Pervis was granted an undisclosed sum of money, the building of WVON at 3350 So. Kedzie, and the tower in the back.

After they finally got the okay, and took control of the license for WVON (WXOL), Pervis got to the point where he had learned how to file applications and things for radio stations because in filing for this license here at WVON, he discovered they all worked basically on the same premises. He filed for a radio station in Memphis, Tennesssee. This was done because then, President Carter was trying to figure out how he could get some licenses on operating radio stations to Black people in America. When President Carter first came on the scene, there were only five radio stations out of 10,000 that Black people owned. It was a travesty, unbelievable. So what he did was to invite a good number of Black folks to Washingto D.C. to find out what was their idea on how to file for radio stations. Pervis was one of the ones invited, and so was Robert

President Carter with Evelyn "Champaign" King

Johnson, former owner of Black Entertainment Television (BET). They
stayed there the better part of five or six days, talking about different ways
to do this and ways to do that. Pervis was not aware, too much, of cable
television during that time; however, he was aware of radio stations by
being at WVON, and he saw what a bonanza could be made with radio
stations. Since he knew how to fill out an application and how to file for a
station, he figured he might as well file for some in some other places.

   When they opened up the clear channel licenses that a person could
file on, providing they protected that same frequency in a 1000 mile
radius during the daylight hours from the city of origin, he found
somebody with a station in New York. It was a clear channel station.
Pervis could file for that same station, if he didn't interfere with anybody
else 1000 miles away from New York. He went to Boston, where the
station was owned, and filed for frequency 1030 in Memphis, Tennessee.

He had to comply and cut his power down at night. When they did get that frequency in Memphis, he had to shoot his signal away from Boston, because 1030 was out of Boston. He had to shoot his signal west.

This led him to file for other stations. He ended up with that license in Memphis, two in Michigan, and Alabama, and one in Arkansas, Florida and Georgia. This went on through the 80s. Some stations were built, and others, he sold the licenses as investments. Pervis was working on acquiring other stations. He built that 50,000 watt station in Memphis, because his dream was for all of his four children to each have his/her own station.

When Pervis first got WXOL, (now WVON) his daughter Melody, the current President and General Manager of WVON would come in and learn the board, while she was in high school. She'd come in and watch her daddy work, and at one time, during her college days, she became news director.

In the meantime, WVON, under the ownership of Combined, was in the process of moving downtown on Michigan Ave., and they did that. WVON had developed a complete new staff and changed the music format. They began to play different types of music such as modern day rap. They cut the gospel back.

Over a period of years, Combined Communications wanted to make sure that they removed all the stigma of Black programming from their station, so they gave up the call letters 'WVON'. Midway acquired them immediately, with The FCC's granted permission. So they changed the call letters on the 1450 frequency from WXOL back to WVON, and became a talk show formatted station, sprinkled, of course, with blues. The first talk show host was Ty Wansley, from 6am to10am Then they would play music, until Pervis came on at midday for an hour's worth of blues before they went off the air at 1pm. WVON came back on at 10pm, at which time Wesley South would host a talk show called 'On Target'. There would be a variety of guest hosts and hostess doing 'On Target' from 10 until 12 midnight, then 'The Blues Man' would spin blues from midnight until five in the morning.

Pervis changed his thinking back to the present. The more things change the more they stay the same. He picked up his CDs and headed toward the studio.

The **40** Year **Spann** of **WVON**

The next afternoon as Pervis sat working, he heard a commotion in the hallway. He was just about to get up and go see what was happening when the door, was pushed open. The Rev. Jesse L. Jackson walked in.

"Well, if it isn't the blues man himself," Jesse said as he extended his hand in greeting.

"Jesse, what brings you here?" Pervis asked as he shook Jesse's hand.

"Jonathan and I are here to do some production work with your engineer extraordinair, Deacon Wayne Fields," he explained. "But you know I had to come in here to see you."

"Well, you know you're always welcomed, have been for the past 40 years," Pervis responded.

"Yes. It's been a long time. When I first met you, it was around the time you had the blues poppin' here at WVON and The Burning Spear smokin'. And all those talent shows you used to throw! I remember when you had the Five Stair Steps, and Chaka Khan; but, most of all the Jackson 5," Jesse said.

"Oh yes. I managed them for five years, right up until they performed the last show at the Regal, before it closed down in 1969," said Pervis. "Have you spoke to Michael

162

Chaka Khan (center)

since you discovered them?" asked Jesse.

"No," Pervis answered. "I don't even know if he remembers me."

"He's going to be in town next week for the National Cable & Telecommunications Association Trade Show out at McCormick Place. His brother Marlon is involved in getting a new television station going for Blacks. If I see him, I'll mention you to him. By the way, congratulations on winning the N'Voice Award. I know I'll be at the N'DIGO gala to see you accept it," Jesse said.

"It's an honor to be chosen. Who would've thought it? Me, coming from a small town in Itta Bina, Mississippi," Pervis marveled.

"I also wanted to extend a personal invitation to you to Rainbow PUSH's 32nd Annual Conference to be held at the Sheraton. I'll make sure you get the rest of the information," said Jesse.

"Sounds like a winner."

"Let me get back around there. I just wanted to say hello," Jesse said.

"It's good to see you. Give my regards to that son of yours," Pervis added.

"I will. We'll talk soon, when I have more time," said Jesse as he headed out the door.

It was always good to see Rev. Jackson. Every Friday night long ago, a young Jesse was on Hotline with Wesley South. This broadcast came about as a result of Dick Gregory. Pervis thought back on a conversation he had with his old friend George O'Hare.

"Spann," George had said, "I was talking to George Jones, of Joe Louis Milk company, and we were discussing putting Operation Breadbasket on the radio on Saturdays. I talked to Dick Gregory, and he said we needed a round the clock station in case a meeting, march, or picket line was called. We've got to be able to announce it at the right time. That means if it's ten o'clock at night, and they decide there's going to be a picket on a company in downtown Chicago, they've got to be able to call that station right then and start telling them about it so that it happens tomorrow."

"That sounds good to me. Why don't you give Lucky a call," Pervis had said.

And the rest is history. Operation Breadbasket would go from church to church and broadcast live, until they got to the Capital Theater, where they took over. Back during the civil rights movement, many churches would not welcome Dr. King, and his arm of the SCLC, Operation Breadbasket, but a few would. Most of the pastors were in Mayor Daley's pocket. One Pastor who was very helpful was Rev. Clay Evans. As a result, it took years to get his new parish built.

From about 1966 until about 1975, or '76, WVON had a special, telephone line for Jesse from wherever he was in the country. He could call on Friday night to tell people to come to his meeting at PUSH on Saturday. If he missed it, it would not be as many people there that next Saturday. Jesse always contended Wesley was the first person to put a microphone in front of him. When Rev. Jackson initially came to town, he visited the station. All the 'Good Guys' were so impressed with him because of his message, that they got behind him and did whatever they could to help. At the time, the Reverend was doing guest speeches at other churches. He didn't have his own church, but they liked, basically, his message: 'you don't have to die to go to heaven. You don't have to sacrifice everything here on earth for what's going to happen in the future'. His message was to help people now, and they certainly liked that.

Pervis remembered one incident that he and Lucky had talked about. The 'Good Guys' had worked with Operation PUSH and Jesse Jackson, and really 'made' the organization. PUSH approached WVON about doing a re-broadcast. They wanted to move the program to another station, WJPC, and they wanted to know if the 'Good Guys' would be amenable to a re-broadcast where that station would carry it, and WVON would have the privilege of bringing to the public a re-broadcast. Mr. Johnson, owner of WJPC called Lucky, himself, to see if they'd be interested in a simulcast since they were not interested in a re-broadcast. They were trying to get the 'Good Guys' to transfer the PUSH program from WVON to WJPC Lucky said, in true Lucky Cordell fashion, that that was not a decision that he could make alone, and that he would have to consult with the people who made the program what it is. Lucky said he would have to call a meeting and speak to the other jocks. Mr. Johnson asked if he could just make the decision himself, and Luciky said yes he could, but he chose not to. He met with the guys back there in the office and asked their opinions and they gave thumbs down on the idea; therefore, no simulcast. Jesse did, in fact, go on over to WJPC. The reason given was that John H. Johnson was a Black man, and he had a radio station. In keeping with the thought of supporting Blacks, he went over there. It was devastating to WVON. Even though the station had been owned by the Chess brothers, it was Black from the top down. Blacks ran it, and made it. Despite this, there was never a problem with the 'Good Guys' and Jesse Jackson. They remain friends today.

The Reverend went on, of course, to run for President of the United States. The Good Guys can't help but feel like they were on the right track trying to help him. Like Rodney had said, WVON was very instrumental in getting, then, Operation Breadbasket, now Rainbow PUSH, off the ground.

165

Rev. Jesse Jackson Sr.

Elijah Muhammed with Wesley

Pervis with Harold Washington

Back in the '60s and '70s, it was not popular to have the Muslims on the radio, but they could always appear on WVON. Wesley South used to have Elijah Muhammed on this radio station, as well as Malcolm X. Any of the radical people that wanted to talk on the air could always talk on WVON. Of course, Harold Washington used to work at WVON. Harold Washington once said he never would have become the mayor of the city of Chicago had it not been for WVON. Pervis, a lot of time, likes to pride himself by saying Harold Washington used to work for him, and he did.

Then, along came a journalist by the name of Lu Palmer. Lu was known for his commentary, 'Lu's Notebook," heard on WVON. He would give an opening title of his specific script for that segment, than an announcer would come in with the intro, accompanied by a background consisting of African drums beating that morphed into a type writer typing. An example of one of his scripts went like this:

167

"Some short takes in the news. This is Lu Palmer

Lu Palmer

with another page from my notebook." (Bongos would begin beating, then the announcer would come in). "Just as the talking drums of Africa once brought vital information to the African Community," (here, the drum beats would become typing) "veteran Black journalist Lu Palmer brings vital information to today's Black Community. Stay tuned for Lu's notebook." A few more strokes of the keypad would lead into Lu. "Some items in the news need some brief comment. One, for example, the World Series is all over now, but I was intrigued when rain post-poned one of the games in the World Series. This made it possible that there would be television time conflict between the game and the debate between presidential candidates Ford and Carter. TV officials did some fast figuring to see how they could manage it if it became necessary so that the debate and the game would not be scheduled at the same time. And y'all know why they couldn't afford such a conflict. Hardly anybody would be listening to Jerry and Jimmy. Everybody'd be tuned to the baseball game. While the time conflict did not develop, but it sure scared a whole lot of folks. It's another little piece in the paper and I haven't been able to get a follow-up on the details, but the skeleton of the story is worth passing on, in case you missed it. According to United Press International, H. Rap Brown is free for the first time in five years, after federal officials dropped charges against the well known Black militant whose name once struck fear in the heart of white America. Rap Brown won his

168

parole, and those of you who responded to the appeal over Lu's notebook to write letters in support of that parole played a role in his winning it. But he also faced extradition to Louisiana to face a 1968 federal firearms charge. The federal officials decided not to press that charge, so 'Rap' is free now. What he will be doing, I have no idea, but H. Rap Brown is a name that will be recorded big in any history of the movement in the '60s. More after a message."

He then would have one of his sponsors, such as The Chicago Urbane League come in with a get out and vote reminder, and conclude with this:

"Finally, we ought not to take too lightly the significance of the guilty verdict brought against two Chicago policemen who brutally beat Richard Lefridge causing him to be blinded in one eye. This occurred way back in February of '72, and Lefridge's case has been knocking around all this time. But Lefridge persevered, and finally two policemen were found guilty of beating him, although two others were acquitted. It's rare for a cop to be found guilty of beating anyone, especially a Black person, but U.S. attorney Samuel Skinner said police ought to get the message that "you can't abuse and beat and mame citizens and get away with it." Well, for many long years, cops could abuse and beat and mame citizens and get away with it. We hope this may be the beginning of the end of this vicious conduct. One footnote- because policeman Victor Howard, broke the code among cops and told the court how he saw these white cops beating Lefridge, the conviction was won. Howard is now under great pressure from his fellow policemen to the point that his

life has been threatened, and the Afro-American
Patrol Man's League has announced that it would
do all they can to protect their fellow officer from
both intimidation within the police department,
and from bodily harm. This is a real
commentary on American life. This is Lu Palmer.

Here, the typing begins again, and the announcer speaks: "For more vital information about the Black community, tune in again to Lu's Notebook, heard Monday through Saturday on this station."

Lu Palmer was and still is a legend in his own time. This godfather of Chicago Black political activisim arrived in Chicago as a reporter for the Defender, in 1950. He was also a writer for the Chicago Daily News, and editor for the Tri-State Defender based out of Nashville Tennessee. For 20 years, Palmer was organizer, recruiter, and precepter for the Associated Colleges of the Midwest, and founded the Black X-Press Info-Paper located in Chicago.

His out spokedness sometimes resulted in him quitting or losing a job. In 1983, Illinois Bell canceled their sponsorship after he became a very powerful supporter of Harold Washington for mayor.

He received his under graduate degree in 1942 from Virginia Union University in Richmond, and his masters in 1948 from Syracuse University. He began his tenure on WVON in the late '80's and remained on until his retirement in 1999.

♫ ♫ ♫

Another popular talent who frequented the halls of WVON radio and thrilled listeners with his prose was 'The Greatest.

Muhammad Ali, who was then Cashus Clay recited a poem for WVON that went like this:

I Am The Greatest
by Cashius Clay

This is the legend of Cashius Clay,
The most beautiful fighter in the world today.
He talks a great deal and brags indeedy,
Of a muscular punch that's incredibly speedy.

The fisted world was dull and weary,
With a champ like Liston, things had to be dreary.
Then someone with color, someone with dash,
Brought fight fans a running with cash.

This brash young boxer is something to see,
And the heavyweight championship is his destiny.
This kid fights great, he's got speed and endurance,
But if you sign to fight him, increase your insurance.

This kid's got a left, this kid's got a right,
If he hits you once, you're asleep for the night.
And as you lie on the floor while the ref counts ten,
You pray that you won't have to fight me again.

For I am the man this poem is about,
The next champ of the world, there isn't a doubt.
This I predict, and I know the score,
I'll be champ of the world in '64.

When I say three, they go in the third,
So don't bet against me, I'm a man of my word.
If Cashus says a cow can lay an egg,
Don't ask how, grease that skillet!

He is the greatest. Yes, I'm the man this poem is about,
I'll be champ of the world, there isn't a doubt.

Muhammed Ali

Here I predict Mr. Listons dismemberment,
I'll hit him so hard, he'll wonder where October and November went.

When I say two, there's never a third,
Betting against me is completely absurd.
When Cashus says a mouse can out run a horse,
Don't ask how, put your money where your mouse is.

I am the greatest!

Muhammad Ali was a constant figure around the station, mainly because he was often on with Wesley South. Pervis remembered one time he ran into to him and James Brown at a Bud Billikan Day Parade. They were all standing on the stand. Pervis had gone through the parade first, then met both of them. Muhammed Ali was, without a doubt, the greatest fighter Pervis had ever seen. They were close friends. To see him standing up on the stand at the Bud Bilikan Day Parade, and standing there besides him and James Brown, and receiving the reception and the things they received was fantastic. When a person does the Bud Billikan Parade, he has done a parade! WVON was part of that parade every year. Pervis has been in it consecutively for 35 years. He has definitely seen his share.

Muhammed Ali was the envy of all the other fighters who couldn't achieve what he achieved. Pervis remembered when he was in the army boxing. He did pretty good. He moved into the semi-pro, than the pros. One day he went to see a guy fight by the name of Muhammed Ali. After that, he came to the conclusion that he should end his fighting career.

They stayed in touch over the years, and Pervis had just about arranged to promote a fight featuring Muhamed Ali, when they suspended him from the ring because he would not go into the army. Pervis had a guy working for him, a good friend by the name of Cecil Partee. He had just about got everything squared away as to where the fight would go on, which was the Chicago Stadium, before everything had to be put on hold.

Ah, the good old days, Pervis thought as he drifted off.

Muhammed Ali

The **40** Year **Spann** of **WVON**

O ne week later, Pervis was awakened by the sound of a ringing telephone.

"Hello?"

"Hello," came the tenor voice from the other end.

"Who am I speaking with?" asked Pervis.

"Michael, Michael Jackson."

"Well, how ya doin'?" Pervis asked. He had no doubt it was him, because of that unmistakable light voice.

"Great. The Rev. Jesse Jackson was telling me about you, and how you were instrumental in getting my career started," Michael explained. "He asked me to give you a call, and of course I had to. I remember all the talent shows my brothers and I were in, but I was kind of young. I don't remember who put them on, or how we came to be doing them."

"I was the manager of the Jackson 5 for five years. Your father and I had a little contract. I would bring you all to town, put you up, and get you ready to perform at several of the local clubs," Pervis told him.

"So you're the one? I always wondered how we got started. I am so glad I called," Michael said.

Pervis went on to tell Michael how they won the talent shows each time, and how he used all his show business connections to further their career.

"Joe can confirm all this," Pervis ended by saying.

"Thank you for all your help," Michael said.

They rang off and Pervis sat motionless for a few moments. What a surprise! He knew Jesse said he would mention him to Michael, but he didn't give it a second thought, that is until now. The emotion gripping Pervis was hard to describe. That little boy singing and spinning, doing the 'James Brown' on stage, some 40 years ago, now a multimillionaire called him to acknowledge him for his help in getting them started. At least this cleared up one mystery for Pervis. It was not as though Michael Jackson had turned into a super-star and forgot where he came from. He didn't even know! He didn't remember the role Pervis played in getting them going! It figures. Pervis wasn't surprised Joe Jackson 'conveniently' forgot to tell the brothers their history.

The history of the wildly popular talent shows Pervis used to put on began with James Brown. After he performed at one of Pervis' shows, he called him to the side.

"Brother," James had said, "why don't you put on talent shows like they do at the Apollo Theater in Harlem?"

"Talent shows?" Pervis repeated.

"That's right," James said.

From then on, Pervis began doing talent shows at the Burning Spear. From there he weeded out the best to compete at the Regal Theater. Hundreds of people used to audition just to be chosen to participate in the contests. Once the Jackson 5 took the stage, the talent shows were taken to a whole new level.   ♫ ♫ ♫

With his mind racing, Pervis prepared to take his morning jog.

As his legs were running, so were his thoughts. Were it not for James Brown, he may have never come in contact with the Jackson 5 at that early stage in their career.

When Pervis first started on radio, James Brown was already singing, and he was smokin'. He had a record out called 'Please, Please, Please'.

Pervis was playing James Brown when he was on WOPA. When he got over to WVON, he then came to realize James was a very, very sophisticated entertainer in the music world.

He was one of those individuals who operated his band and show like they were businesses. James believed that if a person was going to the show to see a James Brown show, that person wanted a complete show, with everybody knowing exactly what they were doing. He didn't believe in any hanky-panky, or showing up late. He had a together band. James was a strict disciplinarian, when it came to having the band there on time, and he made sure there was no alcohol involved on the job. When it came to James Brown, it was strictly business. He operated that way, and he still does, even today. When one goes to see a James Brown show, one will see a show that has been rehearsed, where everybody knows their job and what they're doing. Pervis had never seen James Brown drink anything, and he felt it was a James Brown rule. You had to be 'clean'. If you were singing with James Brown, you had to hit your notes. Whatever was to be done, had to be done in a professional manner. If James had a singer, who could not perform in a professional way, he'd hire another singer the next day to replace him.

The first place he played James Brown was in the Ashland Auditorium. This was one of the reasons he got into the Regal Theater. He remembered a particular telephone call he received.

"Hello, this is Mr. Brant. May I speak to Pervis Spann?"

"This is he," Pervis answered.

"How are you?" Mr. Brant asked.

"I've learned to do without," Pervis responded, in a phrase that stuck with him over the years.

"Let's cut to the chase, You're taking all the acts coming into Chicago," Mr. Brant said. Pervis knew this was true because entertainers would much rather work one night, than a whole week, and he would pay them the same thing for a night as they'd get at the Regal for seven nights at that time. The prices he'd charge would be more, and they'd take in more money . There'd only be one artist on stage. He'd also, of course, advertised his shows on WVON.

"You're booking all the big named artist," Mr. Brant went on to say.   "I

178

Hubert Humphrey with James Brown

see James Brown just played for you and was a big sellout. Why don't you consider the Regal your regular spot? Its got enough seats, and it's conveniently located. I'm sure we'd work well together."

From then on, in 1963, Pervis became the major promoter for booking acts at the Regal Theater.

He'd gotten James Brown by talking with a booking agency, Universal Attractions, out of New York. After numerous negotiations, they finally sent him James Brown. There was a gentleman named Ben Bart. He was an elderly guy that had been in show business practically all his life. He was managing James Brown. He and Ben Bart liked the same things as far as music was concerned. Ben liked big shows because when he played big shows, he got big money. They played James Brown that night at the Ashland, and the place was completely packed. Around 3500 were there. People just couldn't get in to see him. It wasn't too long after that, that Pervis took up his spot at the Regal Theater, and had to call James Brown back to work it. That's when things really went wild. He came in and they worked out an arrangement that James Brown would play seven days, three shows a day. They sold out seven days, three shows a day. James Brown was phenomenal, and a box-office sensation. He came in and did that split and danced across the stage. At first, James Brown would work for no one but Pervis. Wherever Pervis went, James was going to be there, and they were friends. James would come by the house and just visit. If he had a show that night, it wasn't unusual for him to drop by Pervis' house that day. The line for the Regal when James Brown came would extend from 47th street to Vincennes, and also continue the other way from 48th street to South Parkway, then, now known as Dr. Martin Luther King Dr. They'd have a theater full on the inside, and another theater full on the outside. When James Brown came, they would empty the house so that other people could come in. Folks wouldn't leave unless you did that with James Brown. He was so strong. People would stay there until after midnight just to see him perform. That's the reason at the 2000 African Festival of the Arts held annually in Chicago, where WVON is the flagship radio sponsor, over 100,000 people showed up that night to see James Brown perform. Never in the history of Chicago had they had that type of crowd to see an individual in the park. There were no fights or brutality. Everyone talked about what a magnificent show this man still put on, at his age. He was the first Black man to play Soldier Field in Chicago. Pervis played him twice there.

He recalled one of those times he played James at Soldier Field. Some people were trying to sabotage the show, and approached him to try to get him not to go on stage.

James said, "I'm here to work. Mr. Spann already paid me. I can work, and that's what I'm going to do."

And he worked. He saved Pervis' show for him at Soldier Field in Chicago, back in the early 90's. Some were out to make sure that this particular concert did not do what it was supposed to do. When they approached Mr. Brown, they got a complete negative.

He said, "I'll work for Mr. Spann any time or any place that he wants me." James had his back. This made Pervis feel good. A couple of artists didn't show that night because of the hooligan elements that were in the process of trying to make his show fail. They managed to cause some adverse conditions between Pervis and a couple of the artist that they got through to, but as far as Mr. Brown was concerned, he was not one of those individuals. He did the show, and to this day Pervis considers him as one of the greatest entertainers that he ever dealt with in the entertainment business. Not only that, Pervis thought, he's a man. When James gives you his word, it's valid and he sticks by it.

James stood out like a sore thumb because he was always sharp, and people would recognize him. He and Pervis used to work the Bud Billiken parade. James Brown was at more than one parade. Pervis would be on the WVON float, James Brown had his own, or if he were on someone else's float, that would mean great visibility for that float.

♫ ♫ ♫

Three weeks later, as Pervis was getting ready to attend the N'DIGO Foundation's 8th Annual Gala concert and awards ceremony, he went over his acceptance speech he would deliver when he was presented with the N'Voice award, recognizing his major contributions to Chicago.

"Thank you, thank you, for this very prestigious award. It can be said, the true measurement of a person's success can be determined from

Mayor Richard Daley, Latrice and Spann

where he came from, to where he is now. I came from a small town in Itta Bina, Mississippi, not far from where Medgar Evers was assassinated, nor from where Emmitt Till's body washed ashore . . ."

He put the finishing touches to his tuxedo clad body, and waited for his date to arrive, his daughter Latrice. She would be his escort for the evening. Pervis was very proud of all his daughters. His youngest daughter, Chante, would also be on hand tonight, and so would Melody.

Melody has really done wonders as President and General Manager of WVON. Every since she took over, the station has continued to climb and become truly The Voice of the Negro. The Cliff Kelley show, that airs every morning from six until ten breaks ground daily. During the much publicized O.J. Simpson trial, Cliff was instrumental in bringing a different view of the trial to the WVON listeners because he had a first hand update directly from the court room from a journalist by the name of Dennis Shatzman. Every Monday, he would call Cliff, on the air, and give

Spann with award

Spann with friends

Spann, Hermene Hartman and Johnny Cochran

Spann

the WVON family a play-by-play of the previous week's events, complete with descriptions of all the court room antics, facial expressions, and bodily gestures. Yes, Dennis Shatzman was a blessing to the WVON audience, rest his soul. He gave coverage to WVON that couldn't have be gotten from any other source. He even allowed Cliff to use his court room pass one day, and sit and observe the trial in person. Cliff, then was able to bring his own experience back and share it with all.

Another experience Cliff brought back to share with the WVON family was the Million Man March, hosted by Minister Louis Farakhan in October 1994. He had the privilege of attending it right before going out to Los Angeles to the OJ Simpson trial. Talk about going from the sublime to the ridiculous! The great camaraderie shared between the brothers there compared to the obvious racism in the court room in Los Angeles was as apparent as night and day. The trash that was talked in the court room only amplified the fact that the Million Man March didn't even have litter on the ground. Cliff often tells the story of seeing a little boy eat a candy bar and put the wrapper in his pocket.

Yes, WVON continues to capture the listeners attention, just like back in the glory days.

"Thank God for Jesus," Pervis said out loud, as he saw Latrice pull up.

He left the house, got into her Mercedes, and headed downtown to Orchestra Hall.

♫ ♫ ♫

To Pervis, it seemed at this stage in his career, he was either being honored, or going to some sort of convention, gala, or function or other. This time it was the Rainbow PUSH 32nd annual affair. He was going this particular day because President Clinton was the keynote speaker. It was nothing for Pervis to hob-nob with presidents. President Jimmy Carter extended a personal invitation to him at the White House, and of course he had attended.

Driving downtown to the Sheraton, this time, Pervis looked forward. He intended to meet the former president and take pictures with him. He also used this opportunity to plan a concert or two. Yes, after 40 plus years, Pervis was still in the game.

As he entered the hotel, he noticed bodies everywhere. The event was sold out, and people were getting turned away. President Clinton had always been very popular in the Black community.

"Excuse me, excuse me," Pervis said, as he moved through the crowd.

"I'm sorry. We're sold out - oh, it's you Mr. Spann," came the voice at the door to the auditorium, "I almost didn't recognize you. Come right this way."

Pervis was escorted to the VIP section and shown a chair. Yes, he thought to himself. Plenty had been accomplished, but there was much more work to be done. He settled back in his chair, as Rev. Jesse Jackson took the stage to announce the President. Yes, there is more to be done.

That was definitely an affair to remember. Pervis drove home, and once again let his thoughts be his guide, but this time, he was thinking about the past, present, and future.

To Pervis, WVON was more than just a piece of property for the Spanns. It represents an achievement for the Black race, and the Spanns. He thought of his family, his beautiful wife Lovie, three lovely daughters Melody, Latrice, and Chante, and one handsome son, Darrell. He had wanted to build a radio empire for the Spann family. He didn't want it to be just one radio station that the children would fight over. He has found out over the years that throughout life, there are going to be changes among the family structure and he didn't want to create any enemies; therefore, he wanted to build a media conglomerate for the Spanns. He wanted to send one Spann to Georgia, one Spann to Florida, one Spann to Tennessee, and one Spann to Michigan, all working under the umbrella of the Spann conglomerate.

Chante Spann

Herb Kent, Carl Wright Spann with friends

Those were his ideas and he wanted them to work. But on the way, he encountered so many problems. Being a Black man, going into one of these marketplaces that 'they' really don't want you anyway, and have to fight, and fight, and fight, until he changed colors, turning blue in the face, as white folks would say, he thought with a laugh. Sometimes it works and sometimes it does not work, but he just keeps on fighting. That's what a person has to do, the best he can with what he's got.

Pervis changed lanes on the Dan Ryan and with it, the course his thoughts were taking. He acknowledged the fact that he had not accomplished all that he intends to; but, for the lovely family that he does have, he thinks that they are not satisfied. Quite often, when people start to see a person trying to move out of the circumstance that he's in, they're always those ready, willing and trying to find a way to enable themselves to throw a block to make sure he does not break out of that particular

190

predicament he finds himself in. He always has to go back and fight some more. It's just that way in life.

Actually, its been like that all his days, Pervis mused ironically. Every since he left the cotton fields back in Mississippi, there's always been somebody trying to stand in his way, trying to make sure he did not go too far, too fast.

Despite this, he was able to acquire many stations fast, and now they know how to maintain them. He thought of his youngest daughter, Chante, a full fledged lawyer from a New York Law School, and Latrice, the station's sales manager and vice president, also a graduated from Hampton. Of course, she knows how to run a radio station.

Melody, the oldest girl, could easily be the chairman of the board of any corporation she was put on, and do a good job. Darrell, his son, in his way, is coming around to do the things the way that his daddy would like for him to do.

Pervis felt it was all finally starting to come together. He believed, one day, this lovely family of his will reach its Utopia, one way or another, with him or without him, continuing its climb. He knew his girls were so set that they'd have no problem handling things now. They are all smart people, and know how to deal in the world of radio.

He knew this was not the end. One day, this little conglomerate that they have, will reach into the television arena and see where they could go with cable and so forth. The future, as far as the Spann's are concerned, has just begun.

As for the future of Black radio, he had to look at the past. To him, Black radio has become completely damaged by the institution in which we live, America. Under certain administrations, doors are opened and we flourish. Then when they find out how to shut the Black folks down, they try to do that.

The biggest way that they found out lately to shut Blacks down in radio is as the Black owned station begins to grow, someone would come up with some exorbitant, hard to resist figure to buy them out. This has happened to a lot of the Black entrepreneurs throughout America. Thank God they were able to survive that onslaught, and are now looking for other grounds in which to move forward and continue to grow.

191

Melody, he thinks, may just as well have found those grounds. He admires his daughter's vision, especially after her recent purchase of the Soft Sheen building on 87th and Dorchester. Pervis believes it was a stroke of genius on her part. He couldn't hide the grin that covered his face as he remembered the first time he walked into that illustrious structure. It reminded him of the first time he entered the building that had become the Burning Spear. He definitely got ideas. Melody gets all the credit for purchasing that grand edifice. He figures that by the time they get around to doing what they propose to do over there, he'll be able to look back and say she must have really had something magnificent on her mind, and he's with her 100%.

Right now, putting the station over there is in the works, but that's only going to require a small amount of space. The building is so huge, multiple complexes can be installed. It can be used for so many different things. He has to congratulate his daughter for such foresight. He hopes she stays on the right track with the acquisition of other properties.

At this stage of the game, it's almost impossible to decipher the right track for the Soft Sheen building. He doesn't think Melody has gotten all the things together in her mind that she wants to do, so it's hard to tell what they might encounter because when a person tries to move along on territories that have not been explored, she might run into anything. Pervis feels when they run into anything collectively, they can just about handle it. Together they can stand. Divided, if they ever get that way, each can be picked off, one by one.

That's one lesson he learned during his 40 plus years in business. Together you stand. Divided you fall. He also thinks if a person has a sound mind and pretty good judgment, that person can come out with a pretty good plan.

A sound mind daughter may have the same idea as a sound mind daddy, or a sound mind brother, or a sound mind advisor. It doesn't have to necessarily be a relative. There are a lot good advisors out. All a person has to do is find one that she believes in and that thinks along the line of her thoughts. That advisor can become invaluable as far as the business is concerned.

When dealing with radio or television, an advisor has to be kind of a different person because it's best to find someone who can look at other stations, and see where they are going, and try to determine if you want to go in that direction. You may not want to. Overall, Pervis has found its best to get a person who thinks like him.

As he weaved in and out of traffic, Pervis felt as if his life is a huge pattern, being weaved together with different pieces of material to end up as an exquisite quilt to serve as a blanket to cover his family's destiny.

He pulled into his garage, shaking his head at an invasive thought that intruded.   No, Pervis thought, he did not have then and still does not have now any desire to turn over any of his facilities to any individuals other than his family. He wanted them each to have a station in some market place that they could run, and, God willing, his prophecy will be fulfilled.

chapter 1

Cong. Jesse Jackson Jr., Spann, Rev. Al Sharpton

194

Epilogue

What started out as WVON, the Voice of the Negro has grown into the Voice of the Nation.

The daily line up begins now as always with Pervis Spann spinning blues from midnight until 5am. From 5am until 6am, news director Sharon McGhee, aka "The Duchess", hosts First Light. Then at 6am until 10am, World Objective, The Cliff Kelley show airs, hosted by the Morning Miracle himself, Cliff Kelley. Right after that, at 10am, Mo in the Midday, hosted by Monique Carradine, is on until the station signs off at 1pm.

At 10pm, WVON resumes it broadcast with Perri Small hosting On Target.

On Friday nights, Richard Pegue plays The Best Music of Your Life, from midnight until 5am.

Index